Vallejo and the Four Flags

The candle wicks hung from the
spokes of a large horizontal wheel.

Vallejo
and the Four Flags

A True Story of Early California

by Esther J. Comstock

Illustrated by Floyd B. Comstock

COMSTOCK BONANZA PRESS
GRASS VALLEY · CALIFORNIA

© 1979 Esther J. Comstock
Published by Comstock Bonanza Press
18919 William Quirk Memorial Drive
Grass Valley, California 95945
Printed in the United States of America

Library of Congress Cataloging-in-Publication Data

Comstock, Esther J.
Vallejo and the four flags.

SUMMARY: A biography of the man whose life spans the early
history of California under the flags of four different governments.
1. Vallejo, Mariano Guadalupe, 1808–1890—Juvenile literature.
2. California—History—To 1846—Juvenile literature.
3. California—History—1846–1850—Juvenile literature.
4. Mexicans in California—Biography—Juvenile literature.
5. Pioneers—California—Biography—Juvenile literature.
[1. Vallejo, Mariano Guadalupe, 1808–1890.
2. California—History—To 1846.
3. California—History—1846–1850.]
I. Comstock, Floyd B.
II. Title.
F864.V2C65   979.4'00994[B]   [92]   79-21636
ISBN 0-933994-01-X
ISBN 0-933994-07-9 (pbk.)

For
Kim, Aaron, Kellie, Kevin, Dean, Bryan,
Melissa, Adam, LaToyia and Brandon

Contents

PART FOUR:
The United States Flag

Illustrations

Acknowledgments

I wish to express my appreciation to some special people who helped make this book possible:

To Lois Atkinson, who started me on this up-and-down business of writing and cheered me along the way.

To Alma Payne Ralston, who pushed, pulled and coaxed me from rough draft to the final one.

To Myrtle M. McKittrick, whose book, "Vallejo, Son of California," sparked my interest in this extraordinary man.

To Madie Brown Emparan, the widow of Richard Raoul Emparan, a grandson of General Mariano G. Vallejo. Her book, "Vallejos of California," contains many family letters. As heir to these, and owner of the literary rights, she graciously encouraged my use of some of them.

To Tom Gates, Reference Librarian, and Stephanie Borgman, Assistant Children's Librarian, at Central Library, Pleasant Hill, California, for their generous help and interest.

To my family and friends, whose continuing interest has been a great support.

To my always encouraging husband, who consented to do the illustrations.

And finally, to my son, a book designer by profession, who has acted as designer, editor and supervisor of the whole project.

The letters used are quoted by permission of the Bancroft Library, which now owns them.

E.J.C.

Some Definitions

abuela (ah BWAY la)	grandmother
abuelo (ah BWAY lo)	grandfather
adobe (a DOH bay)	sun-dried mud brick
alcalde (ahl KAWL day)	mayor, judge
alférez (ahl FAIR ess)	second lieutenant
alta (AHL ta)	upper
bonanza (bo NAHN sa)	good fortune
buenos dias (BWAY nohs DEE ahs)	good morning
buenas tardes (BWAY nahs TAR days)	good afternoon
caballeros (kah bal YER ohs)	horse riders; gentlemen
cadete (kah DAY tay)	cadet
Californios (kahl ee FOR nee ohs)	Spanish Californians
capitán (kah pee TAHN)	captain
carreta (kah RAY tah)	two-wheeled wooden cart
carretero (kah ray TAIR oh)	driver of a carreta
Casa Grande (KAH sah GRAHN day)	large house
comandante (koh mahn DAHN tay)	commander
contradanza (kohn trah DAHN sah)	Spanish dance
corral (koh RAHL)	fenced yard for animals

del Norte	(del NOR tay)	of the North; Northern
Don	(DOAN)	Mr., with first name
Doña	(DOAN ya)	Mrs., with first name
dulce	(DOOL say)	candy; sweets
Español	(ess pahn YOL)	Spanish
España	(ess PAHN yah)	Spain
fandango	(fahn DAHN go)	Spanish dance
Feliz Año Nuevo	(FAY lees AN yoh new AY voh)	Happy New Year
fiesta	(fee ESS tah)	holiday; party
frijoles	(free HOH lays)	beans
Francés	(frahn SAYS)	French
gatera	(gah TER ah)	cat door
general	(hay nay RAHL)	general
gobernador	(go ber nah DOR)	governor
gracias	(GRAH see ahs)	thanks
hacienda	(ah see EN dah)	large farm; estate
hombre	(OHM bray)	man
Inglés y Francés	(een GLAYS ee frahn SAYS)	English and French
la reata	(lah ray AH tah)	lariat
madre	(MAH dray)	mother
mañana	(mahn YAH nah)	tomorrow
mantilla	(man TEEL yah)	large scarf, shawl
Mejicano	(may hee CAH no)	Mexican
muchas	(MOO chahs)	many
niño	(NEEN yoh)	boy
niñito	(neen YEE toh)	little boy
oso	(OH soh)	bear
padre	(PAH dray)	father
patrón	(pah TROHN)	master
patrona	(pah TROH nah)	mistress
piños	(PEEN yohs)	pines

pirata (pee RAH tah)	pirate
plaza (PLAH sah)	public square
presidio (pray SEE dee yo)	garrison
profesor (pro fess SOR)	professor; teacher
pueblo (PWEB lo)	town
¡pum! (POOM)	bang!
querida mia (kay REE dah MEE ah)	my beloved
rancho (RAHN cho)	ranch
Rancho del Rey (RAHN cho del ray)	King's ranch
reata (ray AH tah)	lariat; lasso
rodeo (roh DAY oh)	round-up
sargento (sar HEN toh)	sergeant
secretario (say kray TARH ee yo)	secretary
señor (sayn YOR)	Sir; Mr.
señora (sayn YOR ah)	Madam; Mrs.
señorita (sayn yor EE tah)	young lady; Miss
sí (SEE)	yes
tío (TEE oh)	uncle
tortillas (tor TEEL yahs)	thin cornmeal cakes
vaquero (vah KAY ro)	cowboy
yanqui (YAHN kee)	yankee; citizen of the United States

Part One
The Spanish Flag

"You asked about the history of
California. My biography is
the history of California."

Mariano G. Vallejo

A blossom of smoke answered him. The shot hit the pirate ship's mast and sent it crashing.

CHAPTER 1

Here Come the Pirates!

LYING FLAT ON THE GROUND, THE TWO boys stared out at the horizon beyond Monterey Bay. Eyes watering, they tried to ignore the cold November wind that ruffled their dark curly hair.

"I see one! I see one," shouted ten-year-old Mariano Vallejo. He jumped to his feet.

The second boy, who was younger than Mariano, scrambled up. He shaded his eyes to see better, and said, "There's another one. They're the *pirata* ships!"

Two sets of sails moved rapidly toward the harbor under the steady wind.

"They're coming! The *piratas* are coming!" From their perch high on the cliff both boys screamed down to the soldiers at Monterey Fort. It was November 20, 1818. The red and yellow flag of Spain whipped straight out.

The lookouts below had seen the sails, too. Figures darted across the beach to the cannon already set up.

Two days ago, an English sea captain had warned the Spanish governor that the French pirate, Bouchard, was approaching Monterey.

The boys watched the ships coming nearer and nearer. Mariano looked for his brother José down by the small cannon guarding the beach. His father was inside the fort.

They saw a puff of smoke and then heard a faint bang. A cannon ball from the larger ship splashed short of the land.

"Fire! Fire!" shouted Mariano at the fort.

Again the pirates fired — and missed.

"Shoot! Shoot!" echoed the nine-year-old, Juan Alvarado.

Just as the boys yelled, the fort cannon roared. Then followed a wild exchange of shots. The boys, frightened, but too excited to move, saw the ships get the range. Cannon balls hit several shore buildings, setting them afire.

"José, shoot!" Mariano screamed to his brother on the beach. A blossom of smoke answered him. The shot hit the smaller ship's mast and sent it crashing. As the ship reeled out of control, the larger one put a tow on it.

The boys yelled and cheered, ignoring any danger. Then, the would-be invaders turned and slowly headed out of the bay. Mariano and Juan raced down the hill. Windblown and breathless, they dashed into the Vallejos' white-washed *adobe* home.

"*Madre! Madre!*" Mariano panted. "We won! Father and José fired on the *pirata* ships. They hit one! The ships turned around and left. We're safe."

"Your father and brother — they are unhurt?" *Señora* Vallejo asked.

"Oh, *sí*. José had them right on target. *Pum! Pum!* He hit a mast. The *piratas* knew they'd better get out."

Juan ran home to spread the good news. Mariano fired make-believe cannon balls with many *Pum! Pums!* Soon his little sisters joined in the din.

In the midst of the noise came a knock at the door. A soldier stood there.

"Pack food and clothing and get out of town. Governor's orders."

"But we won," protested Mariano.

"The two ships have turned for Point *Piños*. Hurry, help your Mother."

Mariano was stunned. "Why doesn't the army fight them?"

"No defense at the Point and too many enemies." The man hurried on.

The governor sent drivers and *carretas* to each family. Oxen drew these two-wheeled wooden carts. They had two ox hides for a floor and two more made the roof. They had no springs and jolted and bumped over the rough roads.

Mariano kept asking questions. "Why do we have to go? Where are we going? Will father and José know where we are?"

"Hush, Mariano," said his mother. "This is no time for questions. Put this packet of dried beef in the wagon."

Hastily, *Señora* Vallejo packed some clothes around

the children in the *carreta*. Soon they joined a group of other fleeing families.

Many years later, Mariano wrote about that hurried exit:

> She gathered around her her whole family, Juana, Magdalena, Encarnación, Rosalia, Salvador and myself. . . . Six blankets obtained from Padre Florencio at Soledad were our only bedcovers. . . . All were sitting or lying, shivering and weeping, cared for by my poor mother. The oxen were hitched to the pole of the wagon at our first camp at Quinado, getting nothing to eat all night.

Mariano and his family had only the few half-roasted strips of unsalted beef to chew on. A few Indians threatened them that first night, but the *carreteros* frightened them away.

The refugees first went to *Rancho del Rey*, now known as Salinas, California. The families living there opened their *haciendas* to them. In the Spanish way, everything they had would be happily shared.

When Mariano's father and brother found them, the ten-year-old was still full of questions.

"It's this way, *niñito*," *Sergento* Vallejo explained. "There are only forty men at the *presidio*. We don't have enough soldiers to stay and fight. We don't even have enough guns and ammunition for the few of us. Spain is so far away that supplies seldom reach us. Even Mexico sends very little."

"But *I* would stay and fight."

"What would you fight with? Men without ammunition are no protection."

"When I grow up, I'm going to change that," Mariano declared.

"I hope you can, *niño*. We need some changes." The *sergento* patted his son's shoulder. "Now I must get back to Monterey and help rebuild the town. Fires from the cannon burned many buildings. The *piratas* destroyed houses and much that was in them. It's not a good place for your mother and you children now."

"Well, it's going to be different when I grow up," Mariano vowed as his father rode off.

Almost a year passed before Mariano's family and the others could move back to Monterey. The governor sent many of them to the San Antonio Mission. The boys

The governor sent many of them to the San Antonio Mission.

and girls, who had been used to army life, liked this new way of living. Even Mariano forgot the pirates in the excitement of so much that was new to see and do.

The Mission Indians at Monterey provided many services for the army post and its families. They made the candles and soap. They spun and wove the coarse wool into blankets. They tended the gardens and cattle.

Here, the refugee families lived in this beautiful San Antonio Mission. The visiting children begged the Indian servants to teach them some of these skills.

One day Mariano and one of his sisters tried making candles. The candle wicks hung from the spokes of a large revolving horizontal wheel. The worker could lower and lift the wheel, dipping several candles at a time into the vat of hot tallow.

"Turn the wheel slower," he told her. "Your tallow drips all over and the candles aren't even."

"They look all right. You're just too fussy," she retorted. "If I do it your way, it'll take all day."

"But you splash the tallow out of the kettle."

"You do it then," his sister said. "I'd sure hate to work for you. I'm going to watch them weave the blankets."

Sometimes the older children tried the carding, or combing, and spinning of the wool. However, none of them were actually allowed to weave.

The boys preferred to gather at a large round basin, dug two feet deep in the ground. Water and fine *adobe* soil were poured into the cavity. Chopped weeds and reeds were added as needed, to thicken the mud.

The Indian workers laughed as the boys galloped

around the basin, churning the mud and reeds into a thick mixture. The boys loved the feel of the soupy mud oozing between their toes. They yelled and squealed as they splashed each other.

When the overseer decided that the mud was thick enough, it was poured into wooden molds. These were about twelve by twenty-two inches in size. The sun finished the job, drying the bricks that now lay in rows. Mariano and the others each put his own mark on the hardening *adobe*.

But all of them stayed away from where the Indians soaked the cattle hides. Mariano and Juan and all the others held their noses as they ran past the smelly hides, drying on fences.

There was no school here and none of the children missed it. As the mild winter passed, they had lots of time for horseback riding. Mariano, like other Spanish boys and girls, learned to ride before he could walk.

He and Juan trailed the *vaqueros*. Over and over Mariano practiced throwing his *reata* until he was the best of all the boys his age. With whoops and yells, they kept the new spring calves on the run.

These sun- and fun-filled days ended too soon for some. Word came it was time to move back to Monterey. When they arrived, many families had a sad homecoming. The homes were repaired, it was true, but many family treasures and pieces of furniture had been stolen or destroyed.

At the sight of still-damaged buildings, Mariano remembered his vow. When he grew up, he'd never let this happen again.

Soon the school reopened, to the disgust of many. Others, like Mariano Vallejo and Juan Alvarado, and a younger friend named José Castro, were glad. Mariano told himself he must learn all that he could. Someday, some way, he'd make his country strong and safe.

The boys loved the feel of the soupy mud oozing between their toes.

Two Ways
to Learn

THE DARK, POORLY LIT SCHOOLROOM depressed even Mariano. Hard, wooden benches lined the walls of the long room. At that time in California, girls didn't attend school. Only the teacher had a book. The boys repeated the lessons over and over.

The teacher was a retired soldier who wore weird, greasy, nasty-smelling clothing. His chickens, running in and out of the room, added more unpleasant odors.

The teacher didn't know much about teaching, but he did know how to keep order. He walked up and down, watching the boys as they wrote letters and numbers. He carried both a long flat stick, called a ferrule, and a whip. On the end of the whip were cords with iron tips.

Spilled ink or lessons copied carelessly brought a slap on a boy's hand. Those who laughed or played or recited lessons incorrectly felt the sting of the whip. Welts and even trickles of blood down a boy's back were common.

The army provided paper for writing. The boys ruled lines on it carefully. When the paper was covered with writing, the teacher returned it. The soldiers then used it for wadding for their cartridges. Paper was very scarce in California.

There were no recesses. However, when a ship came into the harbor, even the teacher wanted to watch it be unloaded. He dismissed school and everyone ran to the beach.

One day the older boys were copying some important papers for the governor. These would be sent to the viceroy in Mexico.

Tense silence filled the room. Even the smallest children hardly dared breathe. The older boys gripped their pens until their fingers ached. No ink must be spilled on this valuable paper.

"*¡Pum! ¡Pum!*" A cannon salute shattered the silence. A ship had arrived!

The teacher was the first person out of his seat. "Put out the chickens and shut the *gatera*," he called over his shoulder as he ran out the door.

The blue waters of the bay sparkled like a million stars. Sun-warmed pines scented the air. All Monterey came to watch the passengers being rowed to shore.

When the excitement died down, no one hurried on the way back to the musty schoolroom. Slowly, the teacher rounded up the last, poky pupil.

Coming in from the bright sunshine, it was hard to see, but the first boys could hear the cackling and scratching. The chickens were still in the room. The *gatera*, or cat door, had not been closed.

"Get them out quickly!" shouted one boy, shooing at the nearest hen. All over the floor were papers, feathers and overturned inkwells.

"Here comes *el profesor!*" called the lookout in a stage whisper.

One glance and the teacher saw what had happened. Furious, he turned on the boys. He ordered all but two into a small closet. Then Mariano heard him order one boy to hold the other while the teacher whipped him.

The boys inside the closet barred the door. They didn't intend to be flogged next.

An older boy shouted, "Let's put *el profesor* on the bench! Let's see how he likes to be whipped!"

The boys in the closet whooped in agreement. They unfastened the door and rushed out. When he saw the boys coming, the frightened teacher ran over to the *presidio.* There, he complained that the boys were threatening him.

Word got to Governor Vicente Sola. He went to the school, calmed the boys and sent them home.

Then he asked Mariano's father to find out if anyone needed to be punished. Poor Mariano! He didn't know what his father would do. But *Sergento* Vallejo rather enjoyed seeing the teacher in trouble. Few people liked him. After all, the teacher should have been the last one out of the room. He should have closed the *gatera* himself.

The *sergento* merely ordered the papers redone by the time the ship sailed. Mariano breathed a big sigh of relief.

Governor Sola visited the school often. Sometimes he

Map of New Spain.

only stood in the doorway. Sometimes he walked about the room, looking at the boys' papers. On these visits, the teacher became quite excited and even stricter. Mariano guessed the governor never told the teacher when he was coming.

Mariano and Juan sat next to each other. One day Mariano looked up to see the governor watching them.

"Like to read, *niños?*" he asked.

"*Sí, sí,*" both answered.

"Want to come to my office with me? I have some papers you might be able to read."

"*Sí, señor. Muchas gracias.*"

Mariano thought even the teacher looked impressed, as he gave them permission to leave. Cocky as little bantams, they trotted off with the governor.

Book-filled shelves lined the office. Mariano's eyes lit up. Books!

"You're related, aren't you, *niños?*" Sola asked.

"*Sí, señor,*" Mariano grinned. "I'm his uncle. His mother is my oldest sister. But we're like brothers, and we like the same things."

Governor Sola spread a large map on the table.

"Here is *España,*" he said, pointing to it. "And here is where we are." He moved his finger across the Atlantic Ocean and across the land to *Alta California* on the Pacific side.

"In 1542, Juan Rodrigues Cabrillo from Spain probably was the first white man to land here in California. Hernando Cortés, who sent him, thought the Americas were islands, just east of India. Juan Cabrillo's orders were to follow the shoreline north to find the Spice Islands, or India. He stopped in a small bay he called *San Miguel.*"

Sola's finger pointed to the bay now named San Diego.

"Cabrillo traded with friendly Indians there before sailing on. Somewhere about this time he broke his arm near the shoulder, but he continued on with the trip. We think he stopped here in Monterey Bay, but stormy weather sent him back to San Miguel. His arm had never healed well. His health grew worse and he died there. He left few records and no one else was sent for a long time.

"Then years later, King Philip of Spain heard England and France were exploring where Cabrillo had been. So, in 1642, he sent Don Sebastián Viscaíno to make maps of California."

"Who had named us California?" asked Mariano.

"No one knows for sure, but Cabrillo mentioned it in his records," Sola chuckled. "It might have come from a book which many Spaniards read around 1510. The book told of an imaginary island near India. A Queen Califia ruled this land of tall black women, like the Amazons of Greek legends. They lived without men and even fought wars. The only metal on this island called California was gold. The book probably made exciting reading.

"It's likely when Cabrillo saw some new land, he decided California was a good name. Certainly the poorly dressed Indians didn't look like the women in the book. So Viscaíno, who had read Cabrillo's notes, wrote the name *California* on the maps he was making."

"Did anyone look for gold?" asked Juan.

"No," said Sola. "The men only went ashore for water and food. They were making maps. Viscaíno sailed as far north as Cape Mendocino. Here they met such heavy storms, the ships turned back home. But Viscaíno made good maps and notes. He named many places. When he stopped here, he named Monterey Bay for the Mexican Viceroy. He said it was the most beautiful and useful bay on the *Alta* California coast. He changed the name of San Miguel to San Diego Bay. Our Monterey probably was his most important discovery."

"Why didn't he say anything about San Francisco

Bay?" asked Mariano, looking at the map. "It's the largest of them all."

"Neither Cabrillo nor Viscaíno saw it. See how small the entrance is? Fog hides it much of the year. Gaspar de Portolá saw the south part earlier, a little over fifty years ago, but didn't explore along the water. Instead, he returned to Monterey. A few years later, Don Pedro Fages saw the entrance from the hills across the great bay.

"But this all came long after Viscaíno's trip. Spain decided to send missionaries to Mexico. They were to convert the Indians and teach them the white man's way of life. Gradually the missionaries moved farther and farther north. Now they have established many missions in *Alta* California. Fages came with Fathers Serra and Crespi. Incidentally, Fages later became a Spanish *gobernador*."

Sola saw the boys were getting restless. This was a lot of history for one day.

"Right now, Spain is having many problems in Europe. She fights with Holland, then England and then France." The governor pointed to each country in turn. "That is why Spain is too busy to send ships with supplies to Mexico and California."

He handed the boys some Mexican newspapers. He showed each boy a place to read and helped him read it aloud.

"Take these home. Read as much as you can. Come again and we'll have another history lesson."

Then, to Mariano's delight, he gave each boy a book to keep.

Mariano burst in on his family, waving his book. "See what *Gobernador* Sola gave to me? It's called *Don Quijote*. Someday, I'm going to have lots and lots of books."

The boys went often to the governor's office. He was a patient, good teacher. Sometimes their ambitious younger friend, José Castro, went with them. He didn't want to miss out on any special attention the other two might get.

Mariano's mother and father liked him learning from the governor. Sergeant Vallejo knew how little attention Spain gave her territories. He knew change would be coming to California before long. He wanted his Spanish son, Mariano, and grandson, Juan, ready for that time.

CHAPTER 3

Of Roots
and Shops

CALIFORNIA-BORN MARIANO AND HIS
brothers were of pure Spanish blood. So
were Juan Alvarado and José Castro. Their
families thought this meant they were
more intelligent.

Most of these Spanish families had come as officials
and built up a ruling class. They believed their sons
should become the leaders under whomever was the
present governor.

Mariano's father traced his family back many genera-
tions. Admiral Alonzo Vallejo commanded the ship
that took Columbus back to Spain in chains. Hernando
Cortés made Pedro de Vallejo the viceroy, or governor,
of the great silver mining province of Pánuco, Mexico.
Mariano's father, Ignacio, came to California in Father
Junipero Serra's military guard.

When Father Serra and his guard reached San Luis
Obispo, Sergeant Vallejo saw there were few women in

California. In 1776 he learned that a baby daughter had just been born to a prominent Spanish family. He wasted no time in calling on the family and proposing marriage. The family agreed, provided their daughter was willing when she grew up. In her middle 'teens she married Ignacio Vallejo, old enough to be her father. In due time she became Mariano's mother.

Mariano inherited something from each of these ancestors. The early Vallejos gave him the love of learning. The admiral and the viceroy handed on abilities to lead and to govern. His own mother was an unusually intelligent woman, and his father gave him a love of the land and the desire to care for it.

These Spanish boys learned more than reading and writing. They went to a catechism class each Sunday where the *padre* made the lessons interesting. Instead of a whip, he carried pockets full of gifts — sweet figs, dates and raisins.

At home they learned courtesy and respect, important in all Spanish families. At the *haciendas* in *Rancho del Rey*, and at the San Antonio Mission they had watched and even helped in practical skills. Someday Mariano might need to oversee his servants making candles and soap and weaving rugs.

These lessons were all important. But the best ones of all came when he would say to Juan, "Let's go down to *Gobernador* Sola's office."

"No ship from Spain has come for nearly a year, now," the governor told the boys one day. "Usually they come twice a year. They bring the special things your mothers want: fans, fancy combs, *mantillas,* and expensive woolen goods."

"I know," said Mariano. "My mother wants a bolt of cloth to make a dress for my sister who's getting married."

"The last ship sold most of its cargo in San Diego and Santa Barbara. Your mothers complained to me that there was nothing left for them."

He told the boys that Mexico now talked about separating from Spain. He gave them the latest Mexican newspapers to take home.

For years Mariano and his friends had seen foreign ships in Monterey Bay. They saw passengers rowed ashore. They saw water and food supplies sent out to the ships.

The boys listened to the passengers telling about the cargo going to Boston, or China or the Sandwich Islands.

"Why can't these captains sell to us?" Mariano asked Sola one day. "My mother wants some more dishes."

"That's one of Spain's rules. No foreign ship can sell any cargo to Mexico or California. Only Spanish goods may be sold."

Afterwards, Juan said to Mariano, "Maybe *el gobernador* doesn't know it, but people row out to the ships at night. My father brought my mother some silk from China for a dress. He got some for your mother, too."

"Maybe, if Mexico ruled us, the ships could stop," Mariano said. "I think *el gobernador* does know. How would Spain find out if he let people buy shoes or ribbons or dishes? He likes people to be happy."

Then one day Mariano had exciting news for his mother. A ship's captain had brought some of his cargo ashore. It was laid out on the beach where people could walk by and look at it.

Mariano watched. Would the governor forbid the people to buy? Nothing happened. Soon the captain had sold out the few articles he had brought.

By the time Mariano was fourteen, more adventurous captains had opened little shops. Still Sola said or did nothing. At first only a few women ventured in. They saw things no mission ever produced or that Spain sent out. They told their friends.

Mariano and some of the other boys hung around these exciting shops. The things from China had pecu-

They saw passengers rowed ashore; water and food were sent out to the ship.

liar smells. These shopkeepers spoke many languages. They told tales of far off lands and strange cities.

Governor Sola stopped Mariano one day. "Would you like to work in one of these shops? Mr. Hartnell, a man from Boston, said he could use you."

"*Sí, señor*," said Mariano, "but I can't speak *Inglés*."

"He speaks some of our language. You could learn *Inglés* from him. Also he can teach you how to keep books and do more difficult arithmetic."

"Could Juan and José work, too?"

"I'm sure I can find places for them if they wish," said the governor. He already knew the shop owners were willing.

Mariano told his friends about the offer. They, too, wanted to see more of these tantalizing foreign shops.

Hartnell took a special interest in Mariano. He taught him English and loaned him books. Because these were not religious books, they were forbidden by the Church. This made his parents uneasy, but they let him read them. Since Mariano learned languages easily, Hartnell taught him to read French and Latin.

Mariano helped Hartnell, too. He knew the local customs and most of the people. His friendly and courteous manners brought lots of business to the store.

No other boys were getting this kind of education. But no other boys were as interested in learning as Mariano Vallejo and Juan Alvarado and José Castro.

The governor gave them more and more papers and pamphlets to read. They knew Spain was now really at war in Europe. She had neither time nor money for her colonies.

A rider from Mexico strode into the governor's office one day. An excited Mariano saw him slap his dispatch case on the desk and announce:

"Mexico has declared herself free from Spain. Mexico claims all of the California territory!"

On April 11, 1822, Mariano, standing straight and tall, watched with all of Monterey as the army lowered the Spanish flag. The new green, white and red Mexican flag rippled proudly in the crisp breeze. The garrison, in its colorful red and black uniforms, snapped to attention. Tingles went up and down Mariano's back as the cannon fired twenty-one rounds in salute.

Thrilled, he thought Mexico might keep the army better prepared. Maybe now they could stay and fight. Perhaps Mexico would make a better, stronger California.

Part Two
The Mexican Flag

Mexican Army Barracks at Monterey.

CHAPTER 4

The New Cadet

B ELLS CHIMED AND CANNONS BOOMED. From parties and dances, the people of Monterey spilled into the night.

"*Feliz Año Nuevo,* Juan!" Mariano shouted. "The bells are ringing for me — I'm in!"

Juan Alvarado shouted back at his uncle. "*Feliz Año Nuevo* yourself! But what are you in?"

"The army, of course." Long ago Mariano, Juan and José had decided to join the army when they became old enough. "I applied yesterday."

"Maybe you won't be accepted."

"I was." Mariano strutted a little. "I heard yesterday."

"All in one day? That's impossible."

"Beginning January 1, 1824." Mariano was so positive Juan could not doubt him.

"I know why — it's because your father and brother are officers."

"Perhaps," agreed Mariano. He, too, had been surprised to hear so soon. "But I'll make good. I'm going to be the best *cadete.*"

"Why do you always work harder than anyone else?"

Juan, too, worked hard, but most of their friends liked parties better than extra work.

"I guess I'm just made that way." Mariano had never forgotten his fright at seeing the people of Monterey flee from the pirates. Now, more than ever, he wanted a part in making California's defense strong. He didn't say it though. Juan might laugh at him.

"All right, *cadete*. Work all you like. But I'm cold. Let's go back to the party."

Mariano was fifteen-and-a-half, now. Most boys of Spanish background chose their careers by the time they were sixteen. Some entered the work of the Church. Sons of large land owners preferred to continue with the family holdings. Many, like Mariano, decided on the army. It offered excitement and a chance to become important. Many of the politicians came from this group.

He waited impatiently for his induction. It seemed to him Mexico was running the country no better than Spain had. California-born Luis Argüello had replaced Sola as acting governor, but the north bound ships still brought few supplies. Mariano just knew things would be better once he became a *cadete*.

At last Mariano Guadalupe Vallejo became a *cadete* in the Monterey Company of the Mexican Army. He put on the regulation dark shirt, pants and shoes. They didn't fit well, but the red cape made a dashing cover.

"How do I look?" he demanded of his older brother.

José laughed at him. "Just like all the other *cadetes*."

"But I'm going to be the best." Mariano had been waiting for this day since he was ten. If he had taken his schooling more seriously than the others and worked harder, it was because he had a goal.

A short time after the induction, Governor Argüello ordered Vallejo to report to him. Somewhat puzzled, he entered the familiar office and stood at attention.

Argüello looked up from the paper in his hand. "I understand you speak *Inglés y Francés* and worked with the shopkeepers?"

"*Sí, señor.*" Mariano wondered what this had to do with the army.

"Also, that you write a fine hand for your age?"

"*Sí, señor.*" What did writing have to do with guarding California?

Argüello waved the paper in his hand. "*Gobernador* Sola left this note for me. He said you knew about the affairs of this office."

Mariano hesitated. "*Sí, señor.*" What was this leading to?

"*Cadete* Vallejo, I'm assigning you to be my personal *secretario.*" He saw Mariano's stricken look. "You don't like that?"

"No — well —" Mariano stood at stiff attention. "*Sí, señor*, it's all right. It's just that — well — it's not what I joined the army to do."

"Oh? And what do you want to do?"

Mariano stuttered a bit. He knew he wasn't supposed to talk to the governor like this. "It's — it's just that — I — I want to help guard California — from *piratas* — and — and *Indios* and . . ." Mariano's voice trailed off. "*Sí, señor.* I will be your *secretario.*"

Governor Argüello nodded his approval. "Sola said

you were not only well educated, but intelligent and well mannered. Don't worry, young man. You'll get your turn at soldiering. Right now I need you. I must send many reports to Mexico. The new laws must be made public. Report to me next Monday. Dismissed."

In the next few months Mariano met important men who came to do business with the governor. He wrote all of Argüello's letters. He learned of Mexico's new policy allowing foreign ships to trade in all ports. Exciting days — but Mariano preferred the army to politics.

Soon, though, Mariano was released to go with other soldiers on patrols. In the following months the ambitious, hard-working cadet moved up the ranks until he became an *alférez*. Now he led his own group, generally ten or fifteen men as needed. They recovered stolen horses and cattle. There were no pirates to chase, but they returned escaped Indians to the missions.

In Father Serra's time, the Franciscan *padres* had enticed the California Indians to the missions with gifts of cloth and beads. At first they were treated gently — fed, clothed and taught religion.

Over the years, the *padres* began to demand more and more work — enforced by whippings — from these once free people. Often the more rebellious Indians escaped to their families or nearby tribes. Then the mission *padre* demanded that the army patrol hunt for them and bring them back.

This was not quite Mariano's idea of building a stronger California, but it was part of his work.

CHAPTER 5

How Estanislaus Outwitted Mariano

ARIANO RETURNED FROM ONE SUCH successful patrol in 1829. They had recovered more horses than usual. Although not yet twenty-two, he set a standard of success that the other officers found hard to match. A messenger handed him an order from the *comandante* in Yerba Buena that pleased him.

Ignacio Martínez, the *comandante,* was the protector of all the northern missions and *ranchos.* He received complaints weekly from the ranchers near the Valley of the Tulares, an area east of Monterey. They told of continual raids by a large band of Indians. Martínez ordered Mariano to break up this band and recover as many of the horses as possible.

The leader of the band, an Indian named Estanislaus, had escaped from the San José Mission. Raised and trained there, the *padres* considered him highly intelligent.

When he ran away, he joined a fugitive from the Santa Clara Mission. Together they gathered thousands of Mariposa Indians in the Valley of the Tulares, by the River of the Lakisamnis. Estanislaus and his friend trained and armed them. They encouraged the Indians to steal food and horses from the nearby *ranchos*.

One small group sent by the army had been unsuccessful. The cannon had exploded and ammunition run out. This group would join Mariano's and lead him to the area.

Carefully, Mariano read the report of the leader of the first patrol, *Alférez* Sanchez. In it he told of the Indians being well protected in the woods beside the river. Sanchez warned of Estanislaus's cunning and intelligence.

Resolved to learn from Sanchez's misfortune, Mariano made out his order for supplies. He would take two cannon, not one. He would double the ammunition he normally carried. As usual, he planned this expedition carefully. More food and medical supplies than he thought necessary for a week went on the list.

As they set out to meet Sanchez, Mariano was satisfied with his plans. This would be the largest group he had led so far: about one hundred and ten. There were older men in Sanchez's party, and he hoped they would accept him for a leader.

The two groups met along the road to the river. Mariano saw Sanchez's men raise their eyebrows — unhappy with so young a leader. He decided he must show no hesitation in any action.

"*Alférez* Vallejo, do not underestimate this *hombre*," warned Sanchez.

Mariano snapped: "I have read your report, *Alférez* Sanchez." Then, more courteously, "He was lucky your cannon exploded. We are well prepared this time."

Just before dawn, a scout saw horses being led into a grove of trees. Quietly, several soldiers slipped through the river mists into the woods. Soon, they returned with fourteen whinnying horses. The men reported the *corral* unguarded and no signs of Indians.

As the troops filed into the vacant area, an arrow pinged into a nearby oak tree. The men scattered. Mariano, furious at his own lack of caution, slipped behind a tree.

"Set a fire around the grove," he ordered. He'd flush Estanislaus out.

Eyes running and smarting, lungs choking with smoke, the men rushed the burned area. There were no Indians. Deep trenches showed the enemy's escape route to the river.

"Search along the river." This Estanislaus *was* well prepared. Scouts traced the Indians to another section of the woods some distance away.

Mariano felt prickles up and down his spine as they came to the new part. He imagined the men felt the same way. Every tree, every bush suggested an unseen Indian.

"Perhaps the cannon, now?" suggested Sanchez.

"Of course." Mariano chided himself for not thinking of it first. He'd never needed one before. He remembered when the cannon balls fell on Monterey. He

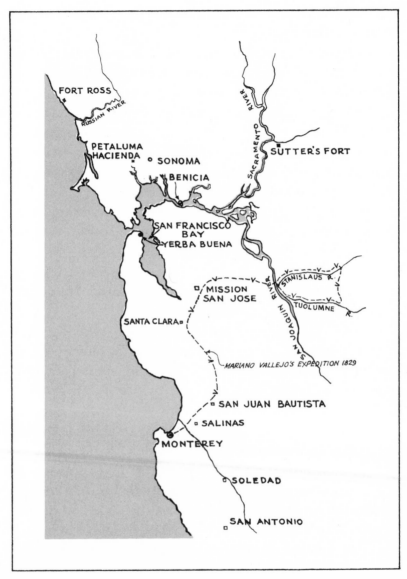

Map of Alta California; broken line shows route of Vallejo's
expedition in pursuit of the Mariposa Indians.

remembered his brother José's shot smashing the mast of the pirate ship.

"Prepare the cannon," he ordered. His mouth was dry and he licked his lips. Would this cannon blow up? But he mustn't hesitate — the men were watching him expectantly.

"Fire!"

The once peaceful woods exploded. Branches and leaves blew high. Frightened, screeching birds flew off. Rabbits dashed for safety.

Ears ringing, the men charged the woods. The best marksmen picked off a few Indians scurrying up the far river bank. But Estanislaus and his men were gone.

Darkness fell. Mariano slept little that night. Where had he gone wrong, he wondered? This was no ordinary patrol work.

Crossing the river the next morning, they found more trenches. The hunt, shoot and run fight continued two more days. One of the captured fugitive Indians hinted of rafts going down the river.

Mariano sent a picked group of runners to see if it was true. All they found were floating bundles of grass tied together. But scouts reported seeing Indians fleeing in many directions.

With the large Indian group scattered and the ammunition about gone, Mariano ordered the men home. Praise was heaped on Mariano for he had also recovered many horses. But he was depressed. He had not captured Estanislaus. In fact, the *Rio de Los Laquisimes* soon came to be called *Rio Estanislaus* or Stanislaus River.

A new and confusing thought plagued Mariano. Perhaps these Indians could think and plan as well as the white men. While he pondered this strange idea, he trained his men even more energetically. If California was to be kept safe from the "thieving savages," he and his troops must be better prepared.

CHAPTER 6

Fortune Smiles on Mariano

AFTER AN EVENING PARTY, JUAN AND José spent the night with Mariano. By now all three were officers.

"The men in my group are grumbling again," Juan complained. "They say the food is worse than usual."

"Mine are angry about their ragged uniforms," Mariano said. "Why doesn't Mexico . . . ?"

"It's the fault of the mission," José interrupted. "If the men had good food, they'd be happier."

"But it's Mexico's fault, too," Mariano said. "No money and no uniforms have come for a long time."

"Let's hope the men don't get too desperate," Juan, more easy going than the other two, shrugged off the problem. "Nothing we can do about it tonight anyway. Let's go to bed."

About two in the morning, a group of ordinary soldiers forced Mariano's door open.

"Five minutes to dress," they ordered.

"Get out of here," Mariano protested, half asleep. "Are you drunk?"

"Get dressed!" This time guns appeared.

Silently, the young officers obeyed. They were forced to join other officers in the jail.

One of the captors spoke up. "We've complained and complained. You'll stay here until the *gobernador* at least gets us better food and back pay."

Before the night was over, older business men of Monterey secured the release of all but Mariano Vallejo and another young officer. No one said why. Many wondered if Mariano had worked some of his men too hard.

In the morning, Governor Echeandia ordered the two released. He sent his secretary, Mariano, south on business. He returned the other young man to Mexico.

Mariano's father had been stationed in San Diego many years ago. Now friends of the family greeted the son and made him welcome. They gave dinners and *fandangos* for this good looking young visitor.

After finishing the governor's business, he had time to explore this city. His father had talked often of his stay here with Father Junipero Serra. The older houses had beautiful gardens. Mariano enjoyed these, an interest inherited from his father.

One day, as he walked past a lovely garden, a movement caught his eye. A beautiful young girl stepped out and smiled. Good manners told him to bow and leave quickly. A young man never spoke to a young *señorita* unless an older member of the family was present. But she was so beautiful, Mariano couldn't move. He had fallen in love at first sight.

He stammered, *"Buenos dias, señorita."* Then bowing formally, he hurried back to his friends.

He asked them the name of the young girl in the garden. He learned she was fourteen-year-old Francisca Carrillo, daughter of a distinguished family. The *señoritas* of Monterey always asked the handsome Mariano to all the dances. But none were as lovely as this young girl.

He had no chance to speak with her, for his ship was ready to sail. So he serenaded her below her balcony one cold January night. He wrote verses and sent them to her when he left.

On the boat going home, Mariano thought of the events of the past two months. Supposing the soldiers hadn't revolted, he wondered. He might never have seen this sparkling young woman! His heart and mind were full of a strange new feeling. Would he ever see her again?

Once more the governor sent him south. This time his friends introduced Mariano to the Carrillo family. Again, he had no chance to talk to this lovely girl, who promised so much with her eyes.

The third time he went to San Diego, he carried his parents' written permission to marry. With this in hand, he asked *Señor* Carillo if he might marry his daughter, Francisca. He was taking no chances on losing this dark-haired, sparkling-eyed *señorita*.

The family — and Francisca — liked the promising, handsome young officer. In the family's presence, he asked Francisca to marry him. The Carrillos gave a large party to announce the engagement.

Then Mariano learned that army officers must have

He had no chance to speak with her, so he serenaded below her balcony one cold January night.

government permission to marry. At once he sent a messenger to Mexico. He asked permission for *Alférez* Mariano Guadalupe Vallejo to marry Francisca Benicia Carrillo, "a spinster of fifteen years."

The messenger had to go two thousand miles by "burro express." No one could guess when he would return.

Back home, the *comandante* transferred Mariano to the cavalry unit at Yerba Buena. This foggy *presidio* contained only a handful of soldiers. Yet they must protect all the land north and east.

Late one afternoon, the ship, *Leonor*, from South America sailed into Yerba Buena's harbor. That evening Mariano heard a soft rap at his door.

"*Alférez*," came a low whisper, "the *capitán* of the *Leonor* has several boxes of books. He wishes to dispose of them before the *padres* find them." The unknown whisperer faded into the mists.

Late that night Mariano rowed out to the ship.

"*Alférez* Vallejo of the *presidio* to see the *capitán*," he called to the sentry.

The captain first made sure the *padres* had not sent his visitor. Then he gladly brought out the books.

"*Capitán*," said Mariano, "I have no money. But I can offer you four hundred cattle hides and ten kegs of tallow."

The captain accepted the offer, glad to be rid of the forbidden books. Mariano rowed home that night with probably the best library in all *Alta* California.

Immediately Mariano sent word to Juan and José to

come see his *bonanza*. They were the only ones of his friends who would appreciate the books. Also, they would never talk about the ones Mariano gave them.

Now the candles burned late into the night. Mariano read book after book while waiting for the wedding permission to arrive.

Comandante Martínez resigned in September 1831. The governor appointed twenty-three-year-old Mariano Vallejo as acting *comandante*. Besides the soldiers at the *presidio*, he was responsible for the eight northern missions and *pueblos*. Happily, he wrote his bride-to-be, "The *comandante's* house is waiting for you. It is furnished with books, books, books. I'm afraid there's not much else. . . ."

The messenger at last returned with the permission. On March 6, 1832, Mariano and Francisca stood before the *padre* and recited their wedding vows. Her yellow satin dress had tiny green ribbon bows on the skirt. A crown of artificial flowers lay on her long dark hair. White satin slippers with turned-up toes peeped out from the long full skirt. A heavily embroidered shawl protected her from the cold spring day.

And Mariano? The *señoritas* ooed and aaed over his white satin waistcoat imported from France.

It was a quiet Lenten ceremony. Afterwards, though, a military band in scarlet and white led the laughing, singing relatives and friends back to the house. A lavish wedding feast followed: *tortillas, frijoles,* roast meats, *dulces,* fruits and fine wines.

Speeches followed the feasting; Governor Echeandia led off with a toast to the bride and groom:

> I drink to the happiness of this young couple whom I appreciate and esteem. I made the young Vallejo an *alférez* of cavalry for his merits and activity in service. I have known his young wife since she was eight years old and have had frequent occasion to admire her fine manners. May Heaven keep happiness for them and may their children be many and worthy of them.

After the governor left, the dancing, feasting and visiting continued for two more days. Young *caballeros*, in colorful shirts and crimson sashes, performed on their horses. The celebration ended when a messenger handed a note to Mariano.

He took Francisca aside. "I must go to the government office in San Diego. *Gobernador* Echeandia says to be prepared to travel."

He held her close in his arms. "I shall arrange for my brother Salvador to take you to Yerba Buena. I will come as soon as I can, *querida mia*," he promised, his lips on her hair.

Francisca's tears had dried by the time Mariano left. The once-pampered young girl was now a soldier's wife.

As Mariano had ordered, Salvador Vallejo and twenty soldiers escorted Francisca and her servants to her new home. The rough little settlement of Yerba Buena stood in sharp contrast to her lovely historical San Diego. But pink Castillian roses bloomed early on the white *adobe* house to welcome her.

The *comandante's* white-washed walls soon were bright with the pictures she had brought with her. Not only beautiful, Francisca had been well trained in making an attractive home.

After the governor left, the dancing, feasting and visiting continued two more days.

CHAPTER 7

Mariano Learns from the Russians

GAIN, IN 1833, MEXICO SENT A NEW GOVernor, unfortunately a man never in good health. José Figueroa asked Mariano to come to Monterey to meet with him. After only a few moments, the two men knew they would be lifetime friends.

"Mexico has sent two special orders for you," the governor told Mariano. "First, the government is worried about the Russians and their plans. Second, they feel we should have another *pueblo* north of Yerba Buena."

"*Sí*, I agree with the latter. There is much land in northern California."

Figueroa gave Mariano two letters for Fort Ross, the Russian post on the coast north of Yerba Buena. One introduced his young *comandante* and the other ordered supplies. Also, he wanted Mariano to learn whatever he could about the Russians' plans for the future.

When Ignacio Martínez had been the *comandante*

at Yerba Buena, he had sent Mariano on several short exploring trips into the northern area. Maps for the coast had shown California extending several hundred miles north of Yerba Buena.

On one of these trips Mariano had seen a beautiful valley surrounded by tree-covered hills. Through Martínez, he asked for a land grant from the governor. The giving of land by Mexico to approved citizens was a frequent occurrence. In a few months Mariano had received the Petaluma land grant, about sixty thousand acres. It included the lovely valley he had admired.

Never, though, had Mariano been sent to Fort Ross. Martínez had told him about the Russians first stopping at Yerba Buena in 1806, though forbidden by Spanish laws. From their base in Sitka, Alaska, they then had settled at Fort Ross in 1812. Here, on the rugged coast, about eighty miles north of Yerba Buena, they hunted otters for their valuable skins. When questioned about its name, Martínez had explained that Ross was from an old word for Russia — *Rossiya*.

Now, Mariano felt a tingle of excitement with his orders. What would this fort be like? How far inland had the Russians expanded to make Mexico so worried? He knew the *Californios* did a good deal of trade with these foreigners, who spoke Spanish. Surely they must be friendly.

Though obviously surprised at Mariano's youth, the Russian commander treated him with respect. Fort Ross amazed the visitor. Instead of the *adobe* brick as at home, all the buildings here were of redwood. Block houses, one seven-sided and the other eight, were at opposite corners of the central square. Their mounted cannon gave protection against any enemy coming from land or sea.

Everywhere Mariano saw hard-working people. Guards stood at attention, never slouching. The grounds were clean, the buildings in good repair. This impressed Mariano.

The small redwood chapel stood opposite the commander's two-storied home. Heavy redwood beams and the dark rough siding contrasted with the Californians' white-washed missions.

Originally, the Russians came for the otter. To care for their fishing and sailing ships, they built a blacksmith's shop. They erected other small buildings where they made shoes and saddles from the hides taken in trade with the *Californios*.

They tried to grow gardens and orchards in the rocky ground. Mariano saw they had moved inland looking for better soil. But half their crops were lost to the gophers. Some history writers say the gophers really drove the Russians from California.

They were the only California settlers to pay the Indians for their land — "three blankets, three pairs of breeches, three hoes, two axes and some beads."

Seeing Indians and white men working together startled Mariano. Also, he saw how well the Indians worked when well treated. Ever ready to learn, Mariano stored these new ideas for future use.

After buying the rifles, cutlasses, saddles, shoes and other supplies Figueroa had ordered, the patrol headed south. At Bodega Bay, about twenty-five miles away,

Fort Ross amazed Mariano; instead of *adobe* bricks, all the buildings here were of redwood.

the Russians had tried more gardens. These, too, failed because of the cold winds and fog. Here, the Russians had an Indian chief and his tribe guarding the bay. Another new idea for Mariano.

Travelling east, Mariano and his group came to a ridge overlooking part of his land grant. He looked long at this richly green valley nestled between tree covered hills. The Indians called this valley *So-no-ma*, "valley of the moon."

This is where I want to live, he told himself. Daydreaming, he pictured the *hacienda* he would build for his lovely Francisca.

But duty came first. He put aside his dreams and hurried back to Yerba Buena.

"I don't think we really need to worry about the Russians," he told the governor when they met later. "They are hard workers, but the land will not grow their crops. Without crops, they cannot stay. However, I'll keep an eye on them."

Mariano then showed Figueroa the maps he had made of the earlier trips for *Comandante* Martínez.

"There are unfriendly tribes in these sections," he said, pointing to various areas. "One of these places might do for a *pueblo*." *Santa Ana y Farias,* now Santa Rosa, was one. The other was on his own property near what is now Petaluma.

"Why not send a few families to each of these areas?" he suggested to the governor. "A few settlers would remind Russia of Mexico's claim to the land."

Governor Figueroa liked this idea. Settlers in a new *pueblo* were offered special favors. Each family was given a small amount of land and money equal to about ten dollars every month. Settlers were loaned a yoke of oxen, two each of horses, cows, sheep, goats and equipment as needed. They were to repay the loans at the end of the first year.

A group of such settlers had just arrived from Mexico. Ten of the families, about fifty people, started north. One group stopped at Petaluma. The other went on to *Santa Ana y Farias.* They planted a few fields of wheat but then returned to the safety of Yerba Buena. As Mariano had said, many of the northern tribes were hostile. The people felt safer nearer a fort.

These unfriendly Indians also made life miserable for the two northern missions, San Rafael and Solano. Though wild horses roamed the hilly country, the Indians preferred to steal those tamed by the white man.

Once Mariano led a large group of soldiers to recover some stolen horses. They caught up with a band of Suisuns, led by a giant of a man. Some say he was six feet, seven inches — unusually tall, especially for an Indian. The two groups fought all afternoon, neither side gaining any advantage.

During a lull, the tall leader signaled he wished to speak with Mariano. Unarmed, they approached and looked long at each other. The Suisun leader never averted his eyes. He indicated that his men would like to join the white man's group. On a hunch, Mariano agreed.

Vallejo often made such quick judgements about people. He had fallen in love with Francisca the first time he saw her. In one meeting, he and Figueroa knew they were lifetime friends. And now he recognized the same bond with this Suisun leader.

The Suisun tribe lived near the Solano Mission. The tall man was their chief, *Sem-ye-to*, "Mighty Arm." The mission *padre* baptized and renamed him "Solano." He quickly learned the Spanish language and customs. Mariano marvelled at his honesty and intelligence. The two became fast friends.

In later years, Mariano and his brother Salvador sometimes had to be absent from Sonoma on business. Then Mariano, remembering the Russians' trust in an Indian tribe, left Solano in charge. He knew the tall Indian and his men would protect the town.

CHAPTER 8

How the Indians Were Cheated

PLAGUED NOT ONLY BY INDIANS, THE missions were now threatened by the Mexican government. The Spanish politicians had left California in 1822, but the mission *padres* had remained.

Each mission, as it started, had received monies from a special fund in Spain. This provided for a few cattle, some smaller livestock, seeds and equipment. Father Serra had planned that as the missions grew, the profits were to be set aside. Each neophyte, as the mission Indians were called, would one day be given his share.

Over the years the missions had flourished. They provided food, candles, blankets and even shoes to the *presidios*. Payment was supposed to come from Mexico, but never had. Now the military and civil officials eyed the *padres* with suspicion. Over 230,000 cattle and 300,000 smaller animals belonged to the missions. No longer did the *padres* protect the profits of the Indians. They sold cattle hides, tallow and grain freely, accepting paper money from Mexico, which later proved worthless.

When Figueroa arrived in 1833, he had orders to disband the missions at once. They were to become ordinary churches. The cattle and sheep were to be turned over to the Indians. The government would take the grazing land. However, the new governor stalled for a bit. He preferred making the change over a period of time, hoping to prepare the Indians for their new liberty and wealth.

When Mexico had sent settlers to the new *pueblo* in the north, no money came for them, as usual. In 1834, Mariano grew tired of Mexico's *mañana* policy. Since the settlers had given up, he took matters into his own hands. He would build a stronghold on his own property, the Petaluma land grant. He would make this place as efficient as the Russian fort.

He chose a spot about forty miles north of Yerba Buena. The neighboring Indians watched its construction with awe. The huge, two-storied building, one of the largest in California, surrounded an inner court. The six-foot-thick walls had openings for guns.

Mariano housed a group of soldiers in one wing. His family and friends could stay in another. Throughout California this place was known as the "Palace."

In a short time, the Petaluma *hacienda* became the working home of the Vallejos. Mariano employed Indians to spin the wool, weave, make candles and tan hides. His many cattle and sheep roamed the nearby hills. In 1834 he requested a brand for his stock. He received it two years later: two upside-down spades with twisted handles.

Requesting a brand was a carryover of Spanish rules. As animals wandered freely over the hills, they mixed with other herds. Only by placing a special mark on each could they be told apart. Once each year, each owner of cattle must hold a *rodeo*. All the animals brought in could then be separated. Since the young ones ran with their mothers, they were easily claimed.

Nearby ranchers came for a few days to pick out their brands. These *rodeos* were times of fun, too. Races and bull-and-bear fights filled the days. Young *vaqueros* showed off their skills with the *reata*. At the Petaluma *rodeos* Mariano entered into the games too, throwing the rope with the best of them.

Afterwards came the huge barbecued dinners. Guitars made music for dancing and singing far into the star-filled nights. Then the ranchers and their families led their animals home to wait for the next gathering.

Early in 1835, Figueroa promoted twenty-seven-year-old Mariano to full *comandante* and *director* of colonization of the northern territory. Mariano knew this meant protecting the northern Californians from the Russians as well as the Indians. Others might be given more political honors but he preferred this. Here was his chance to build a stronger country in his own way.

Mariano joined the governor in Monterey for talks about how to help the Indians. Mexico was now demanding an immediate changeover. Juan Alvarado and José Castro and others met with them. Together they planned how to divide the mission properties. Figueroa asked their help in settling the newly freed people.

As Mariano talked with Juan and José, he felt Juan was perhaps more interested in the plight of the Indians than was José. But both talked mostly about the *Californios* someday ruling themselves. Both were actively working in politics, now. They talked, but it was mostly *mañana* talk, Mariano thought as he rode home. More than ever his new position pleased him.

Unfortunately, Figueroa's already poor health grew worse. He asked Mexico to appoint José Castro as his successor. He thought a California-born governor would be more understanding of the territory's problems. However, Figueroa died before the appointment came. José Castro ruled as acting governor for one month. Then he surprised everyone by appointing his friend, Luis Gutiérrez, in his place. In the year 1836, California had five changes of governor, beginning and ending with José Castro!

As planned, the Indians received their shares of the mission cattle and sheep. Then Mariano watched helplessly as large land owners quickly rounded up these well-trained Indians, who had traded their animals for trinkets and wine. The new owners kept the Indians as virtual slaves. Mariano wondered if this was why José had given up the office of governor so suddenly. Had he disagreed with Figueroa's policy?

Mariano tried to carry out the dead governor's wishes. He spoke to the Solano Mission Indians. "Any, who wish, may work for me. I will write your names in my book. I will list how many cattle and sheep you each have. All new lambs and calves will be added to your account. I will care for them until you wish to sell or move away."

Even with this fair plan, many had traded their animals away before Mariano could list them. Figueroa's sudden death had been a cruel blow for the future of most of the mission Indians.

Races and bull-and-bear fights filled the days.

CHAPTER 9

Mariano's Home and Family

S HORTLY AFTER MARIANO'S APPOINTMENT
as *Comandante del Norte*, Figueroa had spoken
to him. He suggested that his young officer
start a *pueblo* in the Sonoma Valley on Vallejo's
own land. If Mariano moved his troops there, he would
then be nearer to the trouble-makers. Nothing Figueroa
ever suggested had pleased Mariano more.

Mariano immediately began his plans. He knew he
probably would have to pay for it himself. He was glad
he owned huge cattle herds, for he would need many
hides and much tallow for trade. This was just before
the breakup of the missions. He hired many of the
neophytes to help build his home.

He placed his *adobe* house, *Casa Grande*, near the
mission. Then he laid out the largest *plaza*, or square,
in California. Here he would drill and parade his troops.
His home, his brother Salvador's, and the barracks
would be around the *plaza*.

With its completion in 1836, he moved his headquarters here from Yerba Buena. He called the new
settlement Sonoma. The Vallejos' Petaluma *hacienda*
produced much for Sonoma besides cattle and sheep.
Still, many items had to be bought in Yerba Buena.
Foreigners had opened shops there as they had in
Monterey.

In 1836, two of the shopkeepers, William Richardson
and Jacob Leese, gave a large party to celebrate. Being
from the United States, they chose the Fourth of July for
the event. They invited people from all sides of San
Francisco Bay to an American-Mexican *fiesta*.

The *Californios* loved parties and made the opening
of the stores a success. It was an extra-special day for
Mariano, for it was only three days before his twenty-
ninth birthday. Mariano and Francisca took Andronico
II and eleven-month-old Epifania. Mariano's sister
Rosalia went with them. Jacob Leese found another
interest in California that day: a few months later he
married Rosalia.

Three tall sailing ships stood in the harbor. Each flew
the red, white and blue flag of the United States. Below
each was the green, white and red one of Mexico.
Salutes from the ships' cannons roared often.

The men held the celebration party in Leese's just-
completed store. He had decorated it with red, white
and blue bunting and many flags. His partner, Hinck-
ley, captain of one of the ships, provided the music. A
clarinet, bugle, fife and drum joined the *Californios'*
violin and flute. The music serenaded the guests, who
were arriving in boats of all sizes.

The hosts served a lavish banquet. One table held steaming soups and stews. Roasted venison and wild fowl greeted the guests at another. There were many dishes of all the vegetables and early fruits. Great quantities of sparkling wines completed a long-remembered banquet.

Then came the speeches. The Americans asked Mariano to say a few words. He praised George Wash-

The Fourth of July celebration was held in Leese's new store at Yerba Buena.

ington, whom he greatly admired. He said he liked the way the *yanquis* worked and planned ahead. He told them of his dream for California.

He made everyone laugh, though, when he said, "I'm dreaming of a time when I shall ride from Yerba Buena to New York City in a railroad train!"

Mariano's and Francisca's family grew rapidly in the following years. They gave some of their children odd and unusual names. Because Mariano often read books in Latin or Greek, he named some of the babies for characters in these. His first little boy, Andronico, died before his first birthday. As was often done in those days, they named the second boy Andronico II. Then came Epifania, Adele and Natalia. Platón and Jovita arrived after Mariano read Plato's "Republic."

With the eighth baby, Mariano realized that none had been named for himself. Since he, too, was eighth in his family, they named this child Guadalupe, the family's name for Mariano. They named the next two little girls Benicia for their mother. The first one died shortly after birth. Even the second one lived only about five years.

Mariano enjoyed reading biographies, too. The next son he named Napoleon. Luisa Eugenia followed, named for the Empress Eugenia and her son Luis. In all, Mariano and Francisca had sixteen children, ten of whom lived to be adults.

The servants' quarters were near the house. Each baby had its own nurse. The laughing and talking of these and the many cooking, cleaning and sewing women made the home sound like a tree of twittering blackbirds.

The Vallejos often had other children in their home, too. One ten-year-old boy, José Altamira, lived at *Casa Grande* in 1839. It is thought his parents had died in the small-pox epidemic in 1837. Curious, intelligent, and quick to learn, José soon understood the Indian dialects of the women working there.

Playing marbles with his friends one day, José saw strange Indians on the plaza. Instead of lazily sleeping in the sun as others did, these men were talking seriously, heads together. This puzzled José. He crept behind a nearby oak tree to listen.

The Indians didn't realize any of the Spanish-speaking children could understand them. They talked of others coming from the hills to join them. Together, they would massacre the people of Sonoma that very night!

José sat as though turned to stone, too frightened to move. When the Indians finally left, José rushed home. Would his *Tío* Mariano believe him? Heart pounding, he blurted out what he had heard. Mariano listened intently, and then called in Chief Solano. After questioning José over and over, the two men went off to make their plans. They never doubted him, for the boy had always been truthful.

That dark, chilly night, painted warriors crept down from the hills. Suddenly guns fired from ambush. The troops chased the would-be killers far back into the hills. Sonoma suffered no more raids, thanks to a ten-year-old boy.

José so impressed Mariano and Francisca that they adopted him. He became José Mariano Vallejo. They sent him to the same high school and college in Valpariso, Chile, where Mariano planned to send his own sons. Later when José returned to Sonoma, he became Mariano's private secretary for many years.

At Sonoma he laid out the largest *plaza* in California. Here he would drill and parade his troops.

CHAPTER 10

Plots and
More Plots

INSTEAD OF APPOINTING JOSÉ CASTRO GOVernor or recognizing Gutiérrez, Mexico sent a man named Mariano Chico in August, 1836. The new governor ordered Vallejo, as *Comandante del Norte*, to report to him in Monterey. When Vallejo reached San José, friends coming north warned him not to go alone. Already Chico had arrested several important men of Monterey.

Mariano thanked them and returned home. He liked his "Lord of the North" position. He ran his northern post with discipline. If he were arrested, Chico might send someone else to Sonoma. Mariano thought for a few days before he made his plans.

He decided to obey the order, but in his own way. He would go as the head of a territory — with a bodyguard! He chose twenty-two soldiers and ten citizens of Sonoma. Then he picked fourteen members of Chief Solano's guard. Once before, these Indians had startled Monterey.

Slowly and deliberately, Mariano and his men made their way south. The soldiers and Indians wore their colorful dress uniforms. They stayed a few days at the large *rancho* of his brother José. When they left, José promised to send help if needed.

Mariano didn't send word to the governor when he arrived. Instead, he knocked unexpectedly on Chico's door. Always careful of his own uniform and appearance, Mariano was shocked by the governor's clothing. Chico wore a faded dressing gown, a green cap and flopping slippers! Embarrassed, he hastily excused himself and hurried into his uniform.

Mariano seized his opportunity. With great charm he apologized for the slow journey. He told of the dangers of their trip. He explained that he had to maintain the northern territory's defense with his own money, because Mexico seldom sent any.

This startled Chico. Mariano hurried on. He described the Petaluma stronghold. He told of the buildings and plans of Sonoma. He mentioned the Indian treaties he had made — all these for the glory of Mexico!

Mariano had hardly given the governor a chance to speak. Now, he courteously answered Chico's questions. Chico then questioned the guard, especially the Indians. They agreed with everything Mariano had said.

When the governor praised him for his work, Mariano relaxed. He could safely stay on for a while in his old home at Monterey. His little strategy had protected him and his northern territory.

While in Monterey, Juan Alvarado came for long talks with his uncle. He told the same old story. The native-born *Californios* were tired of Mexican governors

— especially this one. Few Mexicans were interested in working for the good of California. To them it was merely a political job, far from home.

"We want California for *Californios*," Juan told Mariano. "Mexico is too far away. Now there are too many foreigners coming here."

"But these men from the United States have ideas we could use. We can learn much from them."

"Yes, but they must become Mexican citizens first. Remember our laws. No foreigner can own land or run a business unless he becomes a Mexican citizen first. It helps if he marries a *Californio,* too. Hartnell, Richardson, Leese — they have obeyed our laws."

Mariano nodded his head. Leese would soon be his brother-in-law.

"Be careful, Mariano. People don't like seeing you so friendly with the Americans. Well, I've warned you. Enough of this. Are you going to the *fandango* tonight?"

It seemed to Mariano there were dinners and *fandangos* every night. *Californios* might complain about politics, but parties came first. Tomorrow, *mañana*, they would do something about their troubles.

Riding home, Mariano thought about how he and Sonoma had changed. His Indian treaties and army discipline had been his way toward making a stronger California. Suspicion and intrigue were everywhere in Monterey, but peace, growth and stability described Sonoma.

A short time later Juan Alvarado showed up in Sonoma, full of plans. He wanted Mariano to join him in a revolt against Mexico.

Mariano listened to him. He remembered the boyhood ideas he and his nephew had shared. Together they had read forbidden books. They had whispered of revolution behind closed doors. They had been young and ready to take on the "dragon."

But now, Mariano reminded Juan, he had a frontier to protect from Indian raids. He was responsible for too many people in the north for him to leave. He treated Juan royally and introduced him to Chief Solano. Then he sent him back to Monterey, with no promise of help.

Back in the capital, Juan set up his plans for making California free of Mexican rule. He sent out letters asking support from loyal *Californios*. In it he implied that *Comandante General* Vallejo would head the military.

A surprised Mariano hurried to Monterey. He knew the promotion was meant to force him to help Juan. Cheers for *el comandante general* greeted him as he rode through town.

Mariano hotly denied any part in Juan's plans. However, he did keep the new title. *General!* Perhaps he could improve all the army posts with Juan's support.

Unexpectedly, Mexico sent notice of new constitutional changes from the laws of 1824. The unpredictable *Californios*, although about to rebel, gave this change their full support. Mariano wondered what Mexico would do about the leaders — especially his nephew, the self-appointed governor.

Again Mexico did the unexpected. In 1837 it forgave all political rebels. More than that, it appointed Juan Alvarado governor! Mexico seemed to be listening to the *Californios* at last.

Mariano visited all the army posts, making plans for strengthening them. When he explained what he wanted to do, Juan said there was no hurry.

"But our defenses are no good," Mariano argued. "You know England and France have been sending men who ask many questions. Either country would have no trouble seizing California."

"You are too concerned with this protection thing. No one has bothered us," Juan said.

Mariano knew his plans were not popular with the army officers either. He guessed that Juan was more interested in staying in power than in stirring up the army. He knew Juan would make a better governor than those sent from Mexico, but he also knew he and Juan would never agree on how to make California a great country.

Reluctantly Juan did agree to one change. Mariano would take care of the area from Yerba Buena north. Juan then appointed José Castro as *Comandante* of Monterey to look after the south.

Captain John Sutter received a grant of land in the great
central valley of California.

CHAPTER 11

Californios
Divided

ONE BLAZING HOT DAY IN JULY, 1839, Mariano stood in his cool tower room — cool because of the four-feet-thick *adobe* walls. He watched a cloud of dust down the road — probably the patrol he'd sent to find new recruits. *Californios* didn't like to enlist. Mexican law permitted troops to seize able-bodied men for the army. Mariano wanted to enlarge the garrison at Sonoma.

At first Governor Alvarado had approved. Lately, though, he had helped some of the new men escape. Mariano knew that Juan wasn't well. He had become fat and flabby, not like the slim Juan of old. Mariano guessed that Juan's secretary, Jimeno Casarin, was making many of the decisions.

Instead of the patrol, three men on horseback rode out of the dust on this sizzling day. Mariano recognized two of them, his brother-in-law, John Wilson, and William Richardson. The third, who rode his horse well, was a stranger.

Quickly, Mariano ordered two cannon shots fired in welcome. The green, white and red Mexican flag was dipped in salute.

Leese went out to greet them. He escorted the three up the stairs to Mariano's large reception room. There, they introduced Captain Johann Sutter.

Mariano stared at this imposing man — sun-tanned, square jawed and erect. He handed letters to Mariano from the governor. Alvarado had given Sutter a promise of land and colonization rights.

During dinner, Sutter said he was from Switzerland and had been a captain in the French army. He had travelled much and had just come from Alaska. He had already asked for Mexican citizenship, in order to receive the land grant.

Mariano thought: Juan sent this Sutter to me because he thinks I have too much power here in the north. He wants my area divided.

"*Señor* Sutter, I would be pleased to have you settle near me here in Sonoma. This valley has fertile land and a great future." This way, Mariano could watch what this newcomer was up to with his "colonization rights."

Sutter thanked his host with great charm. When he left the next day, he promised to think about the offer.

Later Mariano learned that Captain Sutter had received a grant of land in the great central valley. He had started his colonization along the Sacramento River. Indians, trappers and hunters were coming to his trading post, which he called "New Helvetia."

News in the next few years told of Sutter's growth.

He had a fort and several houses and a store. He had formed a small army of trappers and mountain men. Mariano hoped this was only to protect California from any invasion by way of the mountains.

More and more foreigners were coming into California. Mexico became alarmed when Alvarado did nothing about them. Some took out Mexican citizenship papers; most did not. Mexico told Alvarado a new governor, Manuel Micheltorena, would replace him shortly, bringing an army with him.

Californios who didn't enjoy soldiering were pleased — until they learned it was an army of convicts! The Spanish-Mexican tempers flared at this insult.

As he had with each new governor, Mariano gave Micheltorena a bill for the money he had spent in the past years for his garrison. As usual, this governor had no money either. As payment, he gave Mariano the Suscol land grant. This lay along the San Pablo and Suisun Bays, at the north end of San Francisco Bay. The cities of Vallejo and Benicia were later located along these waters. Mariano once said, "Vallejo is myself; Benicia is my wife."

Juan had gone south to talk with others, unhappy at the change in Mexican policy.

"The foreigners flattered Juan with their attention," José told Mariano. "He should have forced them to become citizens or get out. This 'army' "— José spit out the word —"steals from civilians, gets into fights and brawls, and obeys no officer."

Mariano, as a Mexican *general*, gave his loyalty to the new governor. Secretly, he sympathized with José and

Juan and his other friends in Monterey. This saddened him, for as things now were he could see no great future for California.

Riding home, he had the feeling the country sat like a pot coming to boil over a fire. He had liked the first Americans who came and opened stores and bought land. Now there had been English and French surveyors even up around Sonoma. Rough men from the States were drifting down from the mountains. Quick-tempered, they took what they wanted, ignoring the objections of Spanish-speaking people. Everywhere in Monterey there was talk of a United States–Mexican war. The fire under the pot grew hotter.

Mariano took a long look around Sonoma when he got home. Mexico had created this northern post years ago, but seldom had it sent either money or supplies. Without his Petaluma *hacienda*, Vallejo could never have clothed and fed his men. Suddenly, he decided he had borne the cost long enough.

He dismissed his soldiers, sending them to other posts. He would rely on Chief Solano and his men to keep guard in the north. Mariano and Sonoma would remain neutral in the troubles between the *Californios*, their Mexican rulers, and the foreigners.

After this had been done, Mariano received word from José Castro. He said he was ordering all foreigners to leave California. He needed Mariano's horses and men to enforce his rule.

Mariano sent back a messenger to say he had dismissed his troops and would not send the horses. He let Castro know he wanted no part in enforcing José's order.

Shortly afterwards, a rider from Sutter's Fort gave Mariano the latest news. U.S. Army Captain John Frémont had ridden into Sutter's Fort, furious at Castro's order. He had held long talks with Sutter, though the rider could not say what it was all about.

Just before Christmas, a tough group of Americans swept down from the hills above Petaluma. The governor's horses were wintering there with Mariano's. At gun point the men drove off about two hundred horses.

The *vaqueros* who had been in charge of the horses understood guns, but not English. They sent a fast rider to Mariano telling him what had happened. The only words they had understood were "Captain Sutter."

Furious, Mariano put a tight guard over his horses at Sonoma. Who had stolen the others? Sutter was a Mexican citizen. Were the horses for José through Sutter? Or for the Americans at New Helvetia?

A letter from Monterey helped calm the angry Mariano. The American Consul, Thomas Larkin, asked him and Jacob Leese to meet with him and other men from all parts of California.

Larkin made it plain that the United States did not want England or France claiming California. All those present knew war between the States and Mexico was near. Larkin asked the *Californios* to make a peaceful break with Mexico and join the United States. He hoped these men would talk to others in their districts.

Mariano is said to have spoken up. "We do not want to become the dependent of still another distant monarch. . . . In sentiment we are republicans — why do we hesitate? By joining this neighbor of ours, we will be fellow citizens. We can choose our own federal and local rulers."

Most agreed with Mariano. They returned to their homes to talk to their neighbors.

Castro and Alvarado did not agree with Mariano. His boyhood chums wanted no dealings with the United States. Mariano stood firm. Surely this was the only way to make California a great country. He'd ride that train to New York yet.

But Larkin's meeting was too late. The pot that was California started to boil over — not in Monterey, but in Sonoma! *And only in Sonoma!*

Part Three

The California Bear Flag

Fremont ordered the men taken to Sutter's Fort.

CHAPTER 12

Rebels in Sonoma

ON JUNE 14, 1846, THUNDEROUS POUND-ing on the heavy oak front door wakened Mariano and Francisca.

"Open up, General Vallejo! Open up!" demanded an unfamiliar voice.

The roused sleepers stumbled to the window. They saw a group of roughly dressed men shuffling about in the early morning mists.

Francisco was frightened. "Don't open the door!" she warned her husband. "We don't know them. Hurry out the back way and ride to Petaluma."

Mariano calmed her. He could think of no one who wished to harm him. He threw on a cape and went down the stairs.

"You're under arrest," a man told him when he opened the door.

Startled, but still courteous, he allowed two men to enter. He led them into the dining room and offered them brandy.

While they drank, the men told Mariano they had orders to take him to Captain Frémont at Sutter's Fort. They explained they were the "new" Californians, mainly from the United States.

They were forming a separate republic, as Texas had. They no longer took orders from Mexico. They were arresting Mariano because he was a Mexican general.

All this surprised Mariano. Surely someone had made a mistake. Larkin had implied the United States wanted California. Mariano kept these thoughts to himself.

The men, warmed and full of good brandy, grew sleepy. They forgot they were to take the general out to the waiting men. Soon came a second round of pounding on the door. Another man demanded admission. He became angry on seeing the two men half-asleep.

He introduced himself as William B. Ide, leader of the group. He said others from Sonoma would be joining Mariano and suggested he dress for the trip.

Upstairs, as Mariano dressed, he assured Francisca that a great mistake had been made. Frémont was an American and, he thought, his friend. The taking of the horses remained a puzzle. Since Mariano favored the United States, surely Fremont would send the Sonomans back home at once.

His brother, Salvador, and another officer arrived under guard. Jacob Leese acted as interpreter. Although Mariano spoke English, he wanted all present to understand what was said.

Ide gave Mariano a list of agreements to sign. In it they assured the Sonomans no harm would come to their families or homes if there was no resistance. Ide promised his men would care for all the animals. They would pay for all they used.

Mariano had little choice. He must leave his wife and eight small children behind. Andronico, the oldest, was only twelve.

The "ill-mannered, greasy-leather shirted, fox-tailed hatted rebels" demanded breakfast. They killed one of Mariano's cattle for meat. Afterwards they rounded up the horses and ammunition stored at Sonoma.

"See — we ride your horses now," boasted one rebel to Mariano. He turned the horse to show the brand — two upside-down spades with the handles intertwined.

In the confusion, Mariano managed to send a messenger to Captain John Montgomery of the U.S.S. *Portsmouth* in San Francisco Bay. He wrote that a group of Americans had arrested him and other Mexican officers. He asked the American's help in protecting the defenseless Sonoma families.

Later, Mariano learned that the captain had sent his sixteen-year-old son and an officer back with the messenger. They called on *Señora* Vallejo to reassure her. She asked them to sleep in her home, which they did.

When the group of nine guards and three captives left, they took Leese, the interpreter, along as a fourth prisoner. Francisca watched with fear as the group disappeared from sight down the long road.

They camped out at night along the way. As Mariano lay sleeping, a hand touched his shoulder.

A voice whispered in his ear, "Do not speak, *General.* We have surrounded the camp. There are many of us to take you back to Sonoma."

Mariano recognized the whisperer. Softly he answered him. "Thank you for this effort. But we will not be hurt. Frémont will return us at once. Give my love to *Doña* Francisca. Go quickly so there will be no trouble."

Unworried, and grateful for his friends' efforts, Mariano went back to sleep.

When they took the prisoners into Captain Frémont's camp, Mariano stepped forward to shake hands. Frémont stared at him coldly. He ordered the men taken to Sutter's Fort. Several of the guard urged killing the prisoners. It was too easy to break out of the jail there, they argued. A tall, very thin man, named Dr. Robert Semple, firmly opposed the idea.

Furious, Mariano let them lead him away. He had been tricked. He would never trust Frémont again.

Now they were the prisoners of Captain John Sutter. He didn't like having these political prisoners thrust on him. He liked people, so he kept them in a room at his house instead of the jail. He sat and visited them while they had their meals.

Then Frémont turned on Sutter. He warned him that if he became too friendly, Sutter, too, would become a prisoner. Mariano never forgot Sutter's efforts. Later the two men wrote each other from time to time.

Francisca's brother, *Don* Julio, brought Mariano a letter from his wife one day. She had been given permission to write and send him some food. The letter read:

GUADALUPE:

I and the children are well. Don't worry about the family because the men are taking good care of us. We are sad because we don't know when you will come.

My mama sends you many greetings. She says for you to take care of yourself. Your papers are well cared for. I am sending you a little money, a bit of cereal and bread. When you write to me, make the letters well, otherwise I don't understand them.

FRANCISCA CARRILLO DE VALLEJO

Mariano found the money — gold pieces — baked inside the bread. Although *Don* Julio had a return pass, Frémont kept him prisoner, too.

Mariano and the other men listened eagerly to *Don* Julio's telling of what had happened in Sonoma. First the men had lowered the Mexican flag. Then they made a new one of a large piece of white cloth. One of the men painted a red five-pointed star in the upper left corner.

Mariano's five-year-old son had been told to hold a corner of the Bear Flag.

Julio laughed. "In the center he drew a grizzly bear. At least he said it was. It looked to us like a pig. At the bottom he painted the words 'California Republic.'"

Then *Don* Julio became indignant. He said Mariano's five-year-old son Platón had been told to hold a corner of the cloth. When the painting was done, they raised the new flag on the pole. The man told Platón to never forget that day.

"He asked Platón his name. Platón stood up to him; he's your son all right, Mariano. He said, 'I'm Platón, the son of General Mariano Guadalupe Vallejo.' He didn't cry till he got inside the house."

Don Julio told Mariano and the others their wives and children were all right. The "Bears," or *Osos,* as they called these rough men, had demanded the keys to the storehouse. They helped themselves to anything they wished. They took cattle freely for their use.

As far as *Don* Julio had heard, the *Osos* had stayed only in unguarded, defenseless Sonoma. They were enjoying life there. Castro had come north with a small force and defeated a few rebels at Olompali, not far from Sonoma. No, Castro hadn't gone on to Sonoma; the people at Sonoma had wondered why.

Mariano wrote Francisca to send him some packs of paper along with his favorite chess set. He let her know it was hot and sticky, not like the fresh air in Sonoma. Flies and mosquitos flew everywhere. All of them had malaria, he told her.

Francisca sent word to Montgomery that the prisoners were sick. The ship's doctor and an officer went to Sutter's Fort.

Revere, the officer, wrote in his report:

> We were met and welcomed by Captain Sutter and the officer in command of the garrison. All were thick-bearded, fierce-looking trappers and hunters armed with rifles, bowie knives and pistols; ornamented hunting shirts, gartered leggins, long hair turbanned with colored handkerchiefs.

After this visit, Frémont told Sutter that if he went in their room again, he "would hang him on the branch of the old oak tree that is in the corner of the fort." The prisoners were to have NO visitors.

Mariano Guadalupe Vallejo.

CHAPTER 13

A Surprise Ending

N O VISITORS? MARIANO'S HEART SANK. How would they know what was happening outside? How were Francisca and the children?

At first, when the guard brought the meals, Mariano would demand, "I want to see Captain Frémont."

The guard just shook his head. "No talk — no visitors."

The sticky heat continued. They had no exercise except for swatting flies and mosquitos. The doctor's medicine helped some, but Mariano ached all over. He knew the others did, too. Gradually they moved and spoke as little as possible. Mariano wondered if they would just die here. On July 6, 1846, he managed to send a letter to his brother, José, in Monterey:

I am sending you this letter with the object of relieving your mind about the fact we have not been killed, at least up to this time . . .

A few nights later, he awoke from a restless sleep. He

heard low voices and small rustling sounds outside. He roused the others. Were they about to be rescued? Or was this the end?

Suddenly a tremendous bang shattered the night — and the window glass.

Mariano pounded on the door. "We are being fired upon! Let us out before we die in here!"

The door was flung open by Sutter, who was beaming and jubilant. "You are free, gentlemen! Come, look at the flag pole!"

Years later, Sutter wrote a letter describing the raising of the American flag at Sutter's Fort:

For me it was a very important event. Before, under the Bear Flag, my life was in danger and it is a wonder I had not been shot by some of Frémont's ruffians. I had received the American flag which Lieutenant Revere had sent from Sonoma by the courier [July 10], I was walking about because I gave up my last room and bed to . . . two gentlemen.

I told the courier to tell nobody that he brought the flag, that I would have her up by sunrise or before. I went to a few of my employed men to assist me to fire a salute when we got up the flag, which [the salute] was so heavy from two mounted six pounders in the yard that all the window panes where the prisoners were . . . broke all to pieces and then everybody came to see what was the matter and I tell you the Bear Flag men made very long faces. And I went up to congratulate the prisoners and I told them we could now speak free as the great protecting flag of the United States flies and [we] need no more be afraid of Frémont's spies.

The courier told Mariano and the other men that on

July 7, about three weeks after the "Bears" took Sonoma, Commodore John Sloat raised the United States flag over Monterey. The *Californios* gave no fight. Two days later Captain Montgomery landed at Yerba Buena, and again met no opposition.

To add to Mariano's happiness, he received a letter from Francisca.

> For two nights the servants have not slept in my room; the danger is past for a captain from Sausalito . . . put the American flag on the staff where before was the Bear; and since then there are no robberies that I know of. In those days were great *fiestas,* and all of us shouting with pleasure and waving handkerchiefs; but the *Osos* were very sad. . . . I and sister Rosa are not afraid for your life and that of Salvador and *Don* Luis.

Now the prisoners were free — but they must wait for the official papers to arrive. Mariano tried to see Frémont, but the captain had left in a hurry. Impatiently, he watched each day for the messenger, and at last the papers came.

The first thing Mariano had to do was sign a formal statement that he never would fight against the United States. Also, that he would never give supplies and ammunition to anyone for use against the United States. Mariano could not understand why he should be required to sign such a statement; he had *wanted* the United States to take California. Now they were treating him like an enemy. Montgomery understood how Mariano felt. He told Vallejo to forget this paper and act as he always had in the past.

Mariano was sure that California would become a

state, but other *Californios* thought Mexico would take back their territory. His old friend, José Castro, hurried south to join another friend, Pio Pico. After putting up a futile defense, both men, former governors, left California.

Mariano's homecoming to Sonoma was a joyous day. Though still sick with malaria, he thrilled at the new flag on the pole. A sudden excitement filled him.

He brought all his military uniforms into the courtyard. He set fire to them and watched them burn to ashes. He shaved off his military beard, leaving only his sideburns.

His Mexican military days were done, although everyone continued to call him "General." He had a new citizenship — a new future. At long last he had become a *yanqui;* at long last his California had a great, strong future.

Part Four
The United States Flag

Indian summer days lured Mariano out riding again.

CHAPTER 14

Where Is Chief Solano?

HOME! MARIANO FELT LIKE A KING, sitting in the dappled shade of the big oak tree. He took great gulps of the refreshing Sonoma air.

Francisca hovered over him, hardly letting him out of her sight. The children's voices were like music to his ears. The littlest ones climbed in and out of his lap. The head of the family had returned, like one from the dead.

If he thought it was all a dream, he had only to look towards the flag pole. The stars and stripes waved gently over the plaza.

"If only I could have seen them raise the flag," he moaned over and over to Francisca. "If only I hadn't let the soldiers go. They would have stopped that rebel group."

Practical Francisca would shush him. "Don't think about that now. It's done. Here's your medicine the doctor brought you."

Surrounded by loving family and friends, Mariano's

strength returned. Indian summer days lured him out riding again. Afternoons he rested, dreaming of the old days.

"I can't understand why Chief Solano left you," he said to Francisca one day. "Where could he have gone?"

"I thought he followed you. We never saw him after you left. His family and his men said he just disappeared."

Mariano missed Solano, who had been almost like a brother to him. He remembered the day about ten years ago when he had given the chief a beautiful horse and silver trappings. Then he had surprised Solano with forty-four of his Suisuns for a guard. They wore the colorful red and black Mexican uniforms.

Pleased and excited, the chief had given a long speech to his new guard. He told them they must defend Sonoma and the *Comandante*. He spoke so long, that when he finished Mariano laughed. *"Un discurso a la Yanqui.* You make speeches like a Yankee!"

After his appointment as *Comandante del Norte*, Mariano had decided to visit Monterey in his official position. Few in the capital really knew the problems in the north.

In a spirit of mischief, he had suggested Solano go too. Mariano sent letters to people along the way. He told them to be sure to humor the chief. Soon he had received letters of protest from as far south as Santa Barbara. Rumors gave the number from "a few hundreds" in San José to "two thousand savages" in Santa Barbara. From the *ranchos* to the *pueblos*, the people feared any large group of Indians. When the letters begged him not to bring the Indians, Mariano laughed.

Solano and his small group had started out first. A man in San José wrote in his records that Solano's guard "were dressed in feather costumes and fully armed." Whatever Solano had asked for, food or shelter, the people of San José promptly gave him.

Solano paraded his men down the main street of Monterey. The women and children hid behind the bars of their homes. Solano stopped a man who was white-faced with fear. In perfect Spanish he asked the directions to the governor's house.

The maid in a Monterey home wrote that she, too, saw the feathers. She thought the guard's conduct was "very overbearing." She believed them to be "devils loose from hell."

Her *señora* disagreed; she thought they were sent by God as a plague to punish the people of Monterey for their sins.

On this trip Mariano hadn't received his usual warm welcome. He chortled. He had made his point. There were still Indians in the north. Solano's were friendly, many others were not. Mariano still had a territory to protect.

Sonoma roared with laughter when it heard the tales from Monterey. The town loved its giant chief.

The malaria left Mariano, but he still had periods of depression. The United States flag flew, but there was no more action than when Mexico ruled. When it rained that winter, Mariano moped around the house. Then in the spring of 1847, he received a letter from

General Kearny. After reading it, Mariano's depression faded like a bad dream.

Kearny wanted him to be the sub-Indian Agent for the Sonoma-Napa area. The United States wanted Indian affairs settled peacefully.

This had been Mariano's policy since he first visited Fort Ross. One time a warlike tribe had returned stolen horses after he talked with them. Another time, discussion had resulted in the recovery of some kidnapped Indian children, without a fight. Through the years, Chief Solano had aided him and advised him.

However, he remembered best the time when he had gone to Sonoma in 1835 to establish the barracks and his home. He had wanted to be on friendly terms with the neighboring Indians. He had sent Solano to the nearby tribes, asking the chiefs to meet with him.

As Mariano and his small group of soldiers had neared the wharf, they halted in shock. Hundreds of Indians pressed towards them. Expecting a shower of arrows, the soldiers had raised their guns, waiting for Mariano's order.

Then a grinning Solano had pushed through the group. He waved Mariano and his men ashore. He had invited not only the chiefs, but all the under-chiefs and the medicine men. The young leader recognized most of the tribes present. Some he knew were friendly, and others he felt would need watching.

Mariano knew the Indians' love of oratory. Wearing his red and blue uniform and colorful cape, he had greeted them with a long speech. With much arm waving, he told them his government would not take their possessions. They were to stay in their own villages. All would live in the Sonoma Valley as a happy family. He waited as the interpreters repeated the message.

Then Solano had told the milling Indians that Mariano was his friend. He said the white men would help them kill their enemies, especially the Sotoyomes of the north.

They had loved it all. They shouted "Au, au," in approval. "Lerpi, lerpi," meant "go on." More of Vallejo's men arrived just then with gifts, ending the speeches.

Red and blue blankets, and beads and tobacco had delighted the chiefs. In turn, they gave Mariano some javelins and a quiver of arrows.

For eight days the chiefs stayed and more joined them. To be on the safe side, Mariano and his men had camped in a circle around their horses and equipment. The tribes set their camps among the trees.

Amid hoots and shouts, they had played games and held contests during the days. Fresh-killed venison had been roasted over huge open fires for the evening feasts. Patiently, Mariano waited for it all to end.

He had enjoyed the shell-and-feather-decorated dancers, even though they churned up clouds of dust. The sight of them swaying gracefully and chanting "seemed like paradise on earth," he wrote later.

At last each chief made his mark on the peace treaties. After a farewell feast by Mariano, they all had run home with their gifts. Mariano had sighed with relief. Now he and his men could go ahead with the laying out of the new town.

As he had then, he now officially continued his policy of patience and talk in his new role of United States Indian Agent. It was good to work with people who thought as he did. It would have been even better if Chief Solano were here working with him as before.

He enjoyed the shell-and-feather-decorated Indian dancers.

CHAPTER 15

Gold!
Gold!

A MESSENGER RODE UP TO MARIANO'S house one misty rainy day in 1848. He brought an interesting letter from Sutter.

He claimed his men had found gold in Coloma, on Sutter's land. Mariano thought now maybe Sutter could pay the Russians for Fort Ross and the buildings. He knew Sutter bought everything with vague promises to pay later.

Since Sutter also had a lively imagination, Mariano dismissed the news of the gold. But in the next few weeks, more travellers came through Sonoma hinting at gold in the mountains.

When John Bidwell, Sutter's secretary, followed these men, telling the same story, then Mariano believed it. Bidwell told Mariano that Sutter wanted the news kept quiet.

"He fears his workers would leave to hunt for gold. Then his gardens and orchards would die. This would ruin his New Helvetia."

In Bidwell's records he notes Mariano's typically Spanish courteous reply, "As the waters flow through Sutter's millrace, so may the gold flow into Sutter's purse."

Mariano heard later that men ran through the streets of San Francisco shouting, "Gold! Gold!" Yerba Buena had changed its name to San Francisco to match the bay. This simplified things for newcomers.

A boat anchored at Sonoma Wharf a week or two later. It contained wheat, part of the payment for the Russian agents. *Alcalde* Lilburn Boggs called Mariano to see it.

"Sutter has debts here in Sonoma, General. I'll keep this shipment here until he pays us."

"Tell him we'd like to see some of his gold," Mariano suggested.

To the surprise of both men, Sutter sent each a small bag of gold dust. Boggs immediately sent the grain-laden barge on its way to the Russian agents.

Mariano and the *alcalde* decided on a quick trip to Sutter's Mill to see for themselves. At Coloma they found a few nuggets to test. They were real. The two men returned home, their curiosity satisfied.

Gold mining had no lure for them, but they were the exceptions. Workers of all kinds were deserting San Francisco. Sailors jumped ship to join the rush for gold. Vallejo watched Sonoma become a bustling town, rivaling San Francisco. Supply shops suddenly appeared.

He visited with those who were passing through. Some he entertained while horses were shod or sold. Mariano saw how surprised these visitors were at the size of Sonoma. A plan grew in his mind.

There were many newcomers of importance now in California. He sent letters inviting them to visit him. This was *his* California. He wanted to introduce them to it as his guests.

Many strangers accepted his invitation. He wanted them to understand this land. But also he wanted these energetic people to approve of him. They did. They invited him to dinners and balls. Mariano Vallejo loved people, and the *Americanos* not only approved of the handsome, gracious, and generous general, but they loved him in return.

However, most of Mariano's Spanish friends were unhappy about his love affair with the newcomers. They neither came to see him, nor sent him news from Monterey.

The lack of news disturbed both Vallejo and Boggs. A state of confusion continued throughout California, because there were no laws or rules from the United States government. *Alcalde* Boggs was an ex-governor of Missouri. He had a complete copy of that state's constitution. The two men invited others from Sonoma to meet with them and study it. They looked for ways to keep law and order in their town. Later, Mariano heard that other districts were doing the same thing.

The arrival of men from Sonoma one June day in 1849 was not unusual. Francisca interrupted his daily siesta under the oak tree with a call:

"Visitors for you, Mariano."

He rose, yawned and stretched, warm from the filtered sun. Maybe visitors with news from Monterey, he hoped. But these were Sonoma friends.

Mariano and the mayor decided on a quick trip to Sutter's Mill.

"*Buenas tardes,*" Mariano greeted them.

After some small talk, one of the men asked, "Have you heard anything from your friends in Monterey recently?"

"Not from friends," said Mariano, "but my brother wrote last week. He lives outside Monterey, though, and never writes of politics."

The first speaker handed him a paper. "This has just come from Governor Riley's office."

Mariano scanned the paper rapidly. Many California

residents had asked the governor to call a convention. If the United States voted them into the union, California would need a constitution.

"You see, General, this paper asks Sonoma to send three delegates. *Alcalde* Boggs and Joel Walker are going. You are more familiar with these things than they are. Will you be the third delegate?"

As Mariano listened, his spirits lifted. He was needed again. He accepted with the enthusiasm of his younger days.

There was a spring in Mariano's step as he showed his equally pleased guests to the door. His eyes sparkled. Californians were at last beginning to think and act for themselves. They might yet have the strong state he had dreamed of for so long.

CHAPTER 16

Mariano Helps to Build a State

GOVERNOR RILEY CALLED THE CONVEN-
tion for September 1, 1849. Mariano bustled
about with his overseer, getting in the crops
before he left.

Mariano's excitement over the coming convention
puzzled Francisca. What was wrong with a military
government? Spain and Mexico had ruled that way.

Mariano patiently explained. "We want to be a part of
the United States some day. There, the people elect the
governors. Then they elect representatives to make the
rules. This convention is to make plans so that California
can do all this."

Fortunately, the *alcalde* of Monterey had just finished
a new town hall. Schoolrooms were on the lower floor.
The convention met on the upper one. Thirty-seven
delegates came from the north and eleven from the
south. As a group, they showed great respect for the
Californios.

Mariano shared in a dramatic opening. The delegates chose Dr. Robert Semple as chairman. He was the man who had saved Mariano's life at Sutter's Fort. Then they chose Mariano and Sutter to escort Semple to his seat of honor! All three were friends now.

No one present knew more than Mariano of the Mexican rules. Semple made him a member of the Constitution Committee. He helped the *Californios* and the Americans understand each other.

Mariano insisted on the addition of a law already in practice in Mexican-California. All land or money owned by a woman either before she married or received as a gift afterwards should remain her private property. Many of the Americans were against it. They argued it was the duty of a man to take over and guard his wife's estate.

They were voted down by the unmarried men. They felt this law would encourage some wealthy unmarried women to come to California. Thus California was the first American state to provide in its constitution for separate property for women.

There was little argument on one issue. There would be no slavery in California.

Finally, everyone signed the constitution. Immediately the *alcalde* hurried the delegates out. Decorators rushed into the white stone building. Armloads of pine boughs, fresh from the hills, were fastened onto the walls. They draped red, white and blue bunting around the room.

While the delegates waited outside, the *presidio* guns

were fired. First were thirty salutes for the thirty states of the union. Then came the thirty-first shot for the hoped-to-be new state.

Each delegate had given twenty-five dollars to provide a public celebration. By nine p.m. guests began arriving. Beautiful party dresses mingled with the rough clothes of the gold miners. Some even paid fifty dollars for rented patent leather shoes for the night.

Tables of American and Mexican dishes tempted the guests. Stews, venison and *tortillas* sat next to turkey, roast pig and cold tongue. Two guitars and two violins kept the Californians dancing through the night — waltzes, quadrilles and *contradanzas*.

The people of California voted at their first election in November. They would act like a state even though Congress had not yet voted them into the union. They approved the constitution. They elected a governor, a lieutenant governor and two congressmen.

It took five weeks to tell everyone the results. The first legislature met in December in San José. Sonoma elected Mariano as its first state senator. He and Dr. Semple escorted the newly elected governor, Peter H. Burnett, to the platform.

All states are divided into counties or townships or parishes. Governor Burnett asked Mariano to head a committee to divide California. No one knew this young state, from San Diego to the redwood- and Indian-filled areas of the north, as he did.

First they divided the state into twenty-seven counties. Mariano, proud of his Spanish background, suggested Spanish and Indian names for them. He wrote a pamphlet to go with the report. In it he gave the meanings and legends of the old *Alta California* names. This is now a historical document.

The legislature accepted the report with little change. This first meeting was overwhelmed with the work of establishing laws. It defined jobs and named commit-

The convention met on the upper floor of Monterey's new town hall.

tees. But it forgot one important item. It forgot to name a capital for the state.

Then California waited and waited for Congress to vote it into the Union. At the time, Congress was balanced between slave and non-slave states. It almost rejected this brash young land that had been a United States territory for so short a time.

First they passed a bill requiring the territories of Utah and New Mexico not to mention slavery in their laws. Then Congress accepted California — a ready-made state, with its constitution, governor and officials already elected. At last, President Fillmore signed the bill on September 9, 1850, admitting California as a free, non-slave state. With the arrival of the news, weeks later, all businesses closed. From San Diego to Sonoma, there were speeches, parades, feasting and dancing.

When Mariano realized the state had no capital, he acted quickly. He sent a letter to Governor Burnett. He offered one hundred fifty-six acres of land along the Carquinez straits for a permanent capital. With it, he promised $370,000 towards a building fund. Since no town existed there yet, friends insisted he call it Vallejo.

Sacramento, too, offered land and money. Many thought the capital should be in the great central valley. Mariano's was the larger gift, so the legislature accepted his offer.

However, the first meeting in Vallejo brought much grumbling. Buildings were not completed. There were few hotels. Worst of all, there was no entertainment!

Each year they tried a different city: San José, Vallejo (again), and Benicia. Sacramento became the final choice, to Mariano's great sorrow. It had cost him several thousand dollars. But worse, he had not been allowed to make the "grand gesture." His gift had been rejected — a blow to Spanish pride.

Workers of all kinds were deserting San Francisco. Sailors jumped ship to join the rush for gold.

CHAPTER 17

Mariano Meets the Forty-Niners

ETWEEN SESSIONS OF THE LEGISLATURE, Mariano found Sonoma an exciting place to be. Ships coming from the east coast brought thousands of men. Almost all headed for the gold country. Many came through the now bustling town.

Mariano moved among them, interested in who they were and why they had come. All had one goal: to make as much money as they could and then go home.

"I can't believe it," Mariano told Francisca one day. "Most of them borrowed money or sold everything they had to come. And for what? Gold! They are teachers, preachers, storekeepers, lawyers, farmers — from every trade. They think California's mountains are made of gold."

Another day he shook his head as he told her of one man.

"He left his wife and three children behind. He came around South America. First they all were seasick and then nearly died of the heat in the tropics. The meat spoiled and the water was unfit to drink. They got some supplies at Rio de Janeiro. Their ship almost capsized in the freezing storms at the Cape of South America."

"Why do they do this stupid thing?" asked Francisca.

"For gold. He says the eastern States talk of nothing else." Mariano shook his head. "The poor fellow didn't bring the right clothes and he has no money left. Thought he'd be right in the gold area in a day. I loaned him some money to eat and buy what he needed."

Another day, Mariano brought some men home for the noon meal. These were teachers. He wanted to talk to them about where they had come from.

"I saw they were hungry," he told Francisca.

"Sí, but you also like to talk to people who know about books."

Mariano laughed. "I think it was a good trade — food for good talk. But with such soft hands, I don't know how they will ever use a pick and shovel."

Mariano heard of others who came by the Isthmus of Panama, saving fifteen hundred miles. They went up the Chagres River as far as they could. Then they walked to Panama.

One man, shaking with a new attack of malaria, told Mariano, "Never again."

The Indian villages they'd stayed in had been dirty and uncomfortable. They hadn't been warned about this. He had caught malaria; some others had been sick with typhoid fever.

"I'll be better tomorrow," he assured Mariano. Having

had malaria himself, Mariano doubted it. "I'll feel better when I start picking up gold," the man continued.

Once a quiet town, Sonoma now became a boom place for a few years. The need for new supply stores and repair shops provided work for the non-goldseekers. Often they received more gold in a day than most miners found in the rivers and mines.

Mariano and his brother Salvador loaned money to many who were down-and-out. Seldom was it ever repaid. Some came back with no gold. Those who did strike it rich often "forgot" who had loaned them the grubstake.

These were a new kind of Californian. The days of "gentlemen's agreements" were gone.

Much later, Mariano wrote about others who came during these booming years.

> Australia sent us a swarm of bandits [and] Peru sent
> . . . a number of rascals. . . . France embarked lying
> men and corrupt women . . . to San Francisco. Italy sent
> gardeners and musicians . . .

The gardeners saw the good land. They planted vegetables, orchards and vineyards. Gold mines were not for them. They worked hard and became well-to-do. During the gold rush vegetables brought fabulous prices, and eggs often sold from six to twelve dollars per dozen.

The musicians spread out to the cities, towns and mining camps. They were welcomed and filled the need for entertainment.

Lachryma Montis was built of California redwood, with a steep roof and gables like those on the eastern coast.

CHAPTER 18

Growing Pains
in Sonoma

ANOTHER GROUP OF MEN CAME TO SONOma. These were the soldiers of the United States Army. They occupied the old Mexican barracks. These young men interested Mariano the most.

He remembered his own cadet days. He knew many of these soldiers would be homesick, so he and Francisca welcomed them into their home. It was said that the Vallejos' cook was the most popular person in Sonoma.

Some of these young men who lived in Sonoma had names such as William T. Sherman, Henry Halleck, Joseph Hooker and Philip Sheridan. Another young man stayed in town only a short while. A lonely person, he spent most of his duty time at cold, gray Fort Humboldt in the north. Ulysses S. Grant was his name.

While these young men liked home-cooked meals, they found another interest. The general had some pretty young daughters. A story goes that one Sunday morning Joe Hooker and two friends knocked on Mariano's door. He opened it and pretended to glare at the uninvited visitors.

"What is it you wish?" he is said to have demanded.

One stammered, "I — I want to — to — buy some beef cattle."

The other muttered, "I came to buy a horse."

But Joe Hooker said he'd come to see the young ladies.

Mariano didn't change his expression. To the first two he said, "I do no business on Sunday. Come see me again." He turned to Joe Hooker. "Please come in. The young ladies will soon join you in the parlor."

Salvador Vallejo and others took the soldiers on bear hunts. They introduced them to Mexican games.

Mariano opened an old warehouse of Salvador's. The soldiers used this as a theater and put on plays for the town. Mariano later claimed this was the first theater in California.

Government meetings, strange people passing through Sonoma, and soldiers to look after! Mariano became as busy as he had been before the Bear Flag days. Instead of "Lord of the North," now he blossomed as the genial host of Sonoma.

With the increase of visitors, Mariano took another look at *Casa Grande*. It had become too small for his growing family and many guests. Besides, it looked like a Mexican house. The host of Sonoma should have an up-to-date, *yanqui* house.

He looked around Sonoma for just the right site. On a hillside near the town were many clear springs, both hot and cold. The Indians called the area *Chiucyem* after an old legend.

It was said a lovely Indian maid wept bitter tears when her lover left her. She leaped into the spring to drown her sorrow. Feeling he was the cause of her death, the young man returned to the springs. In remorse, he threw himself into the clear waters. Their bitter tears changed to a torrent of joyful ones. The waters cascaded happily to the plain below.

Mariano translated the Indian name into Latin. Now it read *Lachryma Montis,* meaning "Tear of the Mountain." Here he would build his new home.

He planned a house like those on the eastern coast. He built the house of California redwood, with a steep roof and gables. He used the best of the Spanish-Mexican period, too. He put *adobe* brick between the walls to keep his home warm in winter and cool in summer.

For every room he ordered fireplaces with white marble mantels. Iron came from China for pipes. Each bedroom and bath had hot and cold water, fresh from the mountain springs. No one else in California could boast such a luxury.

He built this house twice the size of *Casa Grande.* Elegant Spanish tapestries and velvet rugs matched the carved furniture and heavy drapes. Rumors said Mariano spent about $50,000 for the furnishings.

Mariano once wrote a paper on how to live happily:

[One needs] to have a good home, good furniture, good carpeting, good bedrooms, good fireplaces for fires in cold weather; water in abundance for everything and in addition good and excellent baths; a good kitchen with its accompanying utensils; a great deal of wood to poke, a good dining room; many, many abundant vegetables of all kinds all year round; in season a great deal of fruit of all kinds, always fresh and preserved; chickens, eggs, milk that is always fresh, ducks and geese; a cook, a laundress, etc.

Lachryma Montis answered Mariano's needs.

Nearby he built his storehouse. The timbers were precut in Switzerland and carefully numbered. They came by ship to San Francisco and were put together in Sonoma. He trimmed it with fancy brick from South America. They called this the "Swiss Chalet." He stored wines, olives and grains there. Sometimes he used the upstairs as a guest house.

In the rear, Mariano put in a large brick-lined pool filled by the springs. Water bubbled in a graceful fountain in the courtyard.

Doña Francisca had not been as happy as her husband with the new politics. With bitterness she remembered the treatment she received during the Bear Flag days. But now she had a show place. She loved seeing the astonishment of the *yanquis* at the magnificence of *Lachryma Montis*.

CHAPTER 19

Problems; Then a Big Surprise

TRAFFIC TO THE GOLD FIELDS SLOWED IN the late 1850s. Now, wagon trains with whole families came over the mountains. Often with them came trouble for Mariano and the other Spanish-Californians.

Mariano had always enjoyed early morning rides through the dew-covered fields. Up and down the valley he could see the breakfast fires. These people here in the valley had bought land from him. He thought of them as his people.

On one of these rides he saw a covered wagon along the creek. Two thin, bony oxen grazed hungrily, knee deep in the grassy meadow. The acrid smoke of a green wood fire stung his eyes.

Coming nearer, he saw many patches on the dirty gray canvas top. Torn by trees or rocks, he wondered, or by Indian arrows?

Always friendly, he rode over to greet them. "Welcome friends, where are you from?"

"Indiana," the tall, sunburned man replied. Four young ones skittered behind the wagon. A stoop-shouldered woman coughed and stirred the pot over the fire.

It was a puzzled Mariano who rode home to his own breakfast a little later.

"I met some queer people down by the creek this morning," he told Francisca. "They've come from Indiana. Went by the gold fields, but they didn't find any. The man says he's a farmer and is looking for land."

"Did you offer him any?"

The timbers were pre-cut in Switzerland, so they called it the Swiss Chalet.

"I told him I'd sell him some on the other side of town. That's what is puzzling me. He got real angry. Wanted to see my 'papers' for the land. Said they'd heard land was free in California."

"Free!" echoed Francisca. "Didn't you tell him the government gave you this land?"

"Yes, but he wanted to know why I needed so much. I told him to find land he liked and then come see me. They were queer people. The young ones looked half-starved and the oxen did, too."

"Maybe I should send down some food." It wouldn't be the first time she'd sent servants to those passing through Sonoma.

The two maids returned later that morning saying the family had moved on.

A few weeks later, Mariano rode on business to the other side of Sonoma. Afterwards he rode on up the valley. He came on the same family in a pleasant meadow. The man had already plowed part of the land.

This time when Mariano reached home, he was really upset.

"I found that family again. He refuses to pay me until I show him my title to it. He says if I didn't pay for it, why should he.

"I told him when I sell land to people, I give them a title. But it just made him angrier. He said he was staying."

"Can he do that? That's not honest."

"For years I asked the governors to survey our land. But Spain and Mexico never kept any good land records. In the treaty with Mexico, the United States promised the *Californios* we would keep our property rights. But here is this man just taking my land."

More and more families came looking for farming land. Some paid; many didn't.

Finally Congress listened to all the complaints. It passed a law. The *Californios* were to take papers or anything they had to prove their land was theirs to a committee. They had two years to do this. The committee then would give titles. Lawyers came from all over America. Here there was work for many.

The Federal Land Commission approved Mariano's Petaluma properties. This meant many squatters, or people who lived on the land without paying, must move. They refused to go.

As the man from Indiana said, "Mr. Vallejo never paid for this land. We have built houses and farmed it. We own it as much as Mr. Vallejo does."

If people don't like a state's ruling, their lawyers can go to the Supreme Court. Only Congress can change what this high court rules. The lawyers for the squatters went to Washington, D.C. They asked the Supreme Court to change the ruling that favored Mariano.

Of course, this meant Mariano had to hire lawyers there to protect his claims.

While they waited, Mariano and Francisca had an unexpected surprise. Platón came home to visit. For five years he had been in school in Maryland. Now, at sixteen, he was studying to be a doctor. All the family came to hear Platón tell about his school and life there.

One sunny afternoon, Francisca and Mariano sat on the porch talking with Platón. Looking down the long driveway, they saw a stranger coming. Mariano sat up straight and stared. Something about the walk was familiar. He stared and stared. It couldn't be — the shoulders were too stooped. Suddenly, Mariano leaped from his chair and ran towards the stranger. He threw his arms about him in a great bear hug.

"Solano! Solano!" he shouted to the watchers on the porch. It really was Chief Solano, who had disappeared twelve years before.

Solano's Indian dignity broke. Tears streamed down his lined brown cheeks to mingle with Mariano's.

"*Señor*, I have come to serve you again."

"No, not to serve. To be my friend." Together they joined a smiling Francisca and Platón.

The four talked late that night. Solano told them that when he saw the Bear Flaggers take Mariano away, his world collapsed. He thought the white men had killed his friend. He last remembered Platón as the little boy who rode on his shoulders around town.

"I go far away from white man. I look for tribe that needs a chief." He had travelled far to the north. Then, becoming ill, he turned towards home. To his great joy he learned his beloved chief still lived.

He stayed with Mariano for a short time, visiting his daughters who lived nearby. While visiting Suisun friends in Fairfield, he died. They buried him under a great oak tree there.

Washington, D.C., was a big city to explore, and Mariano had two wide-eyed boys to share his excitement.

CHAPTER 20

Mariano Meets President Lincoln

A T LAST GOOD NEWS CAME FOR MARIANO. The Supreme Court gave him clear title to his Petaluma Land Grant. Then the whole process was repeated for the Suscol grant. This time, however, the squatters won.

Mariano's lawyers wrote him from Washington: "We are taking the case to the Congress. There must be a clear ruling on the native Californian's right. New laws are needed."

Mariano agreed, but it cost a lot of money to hire lawyers. He told people that the bandits who escaped from Australia stole the horses and cattle, but legal thieves (lawyers) took away the land and houses.

He sold lots in Vallejo and Benicia to pay them. Waiting and waiting for news made him feel he was in jail again.

"If I go to Washington, maybe I can get answers sooner," he said to Francisca.

"You go, but I'll stay home." Francisca still remembered those days when she had been surrounded by unfriendly English-speaking people. "I don't speak *Inglés*," she said.

There were only four children at home now. The two youngest, Luisa and Maria, had been born under the United States flag. Their brothers and sisters called them the little *yanquis*. They would stay home with their mother.

"I'll take Uladislau and Napoleon with me," Mariano decided. "We will see Andronico and Platón."

The eighteen- and thirteen-year-olds were delighted. Together with their father they sailed by ship to Panama. Not only were roads better, but a railroad now crossed the Isthmus.

When they reached Washington, D.C., the lawyers had good and bad news.

"People who bought land from you need pay only a small fee. Then they will receive a clear title. It is fortunate that you surveyed the land for each of them."

The Civil War was taking most of the attention of Congress. Mariano's own suit must wait.

But here was a big city to explore and two wide-eyed boys to share his own excitement. Platón, now a surgeon in the Northern army, joined them when he could.

Mariano hunted up the young officers who had been in Sonoma. Sherman and Sheridan now were Union generals, and President Lincoln had just made Grant the top general of the Union Army!

Through Sheridan and Grant, Mariano met many important people in the capital. This tall, handsome native Californian took them by surprise. How could such intelligence, education and courtly manners come from the Wild West?

From all parts of the city he received dinner and evening invitations. He enjoyed seeing the homes and how the people lived. He could trace his ancestry back as far, or even farther, than they could. He wished he could show them *Lachryma Montis*. He chuckled, thinking how surprised they would be to see his rich furnishings. He knew his fine collection of books would amaze them — and especially his piano.

The piano had been a surprise for Francisca. In 1843, Captain Stephen Smith of Baltimore had brought three square pianos around the Horn. One went to Los Angeles, one to Monterey and the third to Sonoma. Years passed before Mariano had found anyone who could teach his family to play it.

General Grant introduced Mariano to President Lincoln. Asked if he liked Yankees, Mariano is said to have replied, "They are a wonderful people. Wherever they go, they make improvements. If they were to emigrate to hell itself, they would irrigate it, plant trees and flower gardens [and] make everything so pleasant and beautiful that by the time we get there we can sit down at a marble topped table and eat ice cream."

Lincoln let him ride on a fast train to the battle front. Afterwards he asked Mariano how he liked the ride.

"The train went so fast, I could hardly see the landscape. I thought I was going to hell. I had one satisfaction — I was going in good style."

Time passed quickly and the war ended. Mariano and his sons were in the crowd that heard the President say, "With malice toward none, with charity for all . . ."

Mariano felt the words were directed at him. It was time to go home. Before he could complete his plans, the country was stunned by the president's death. Saddened, Mariano now hurried his plans. He was anxious to be on his way home to Francisca and the quiet of Sonoma.

Home at last. The family sat by the fireside — gifts to be opened, tales to be told. Francisca's warm welcome said how much she had missed her "men."

"You have grown," she exclaimed to Napoleon. She held him off to look at him.

Friends came often to hear of the people Mariano had met. He described the train ride and his visit with the President. His voice choked, telling about Lincoln's great victory speech.

"Our land problems are still not settled," he warned his friends. "With all Washington mourning his death, no one wanted to talk about our troubles. But I shall never forget those words of Lincoln's: 'With malice toward none; with charity for all.'"

Mariano tried to do as the President had advised. When his family wanted him to protest so much loss of land, he stopped them.

"Laws are made for the good of the most people, not just one person. Forget our troubles."

Still straight and tall, his hair black as ever, Mariano was the center of every state and local gathering. The Native Sons of the Golden West made him an honorary member. He enjoyed the Society of California Pioneers. For many years he was the treasurer of the State Board of Horticulture.

He loved people and they called on him often to speak. Twice, Sonoma chose him for mayor.

People asked him over and over to tell about California's early days. He thought of many things he wanted to tell his grandchildren. He had kept many letters and papers over the years. So Mariano decided to write a book. He would write the history of California up to 1850.

He had left his library in the old *Casa Grande*. He turned one room there into an office. It made a quiet retreat from bustling *Lachryma Montis*. He worked happily for several months. This would be his last gift for his beloved California. When he had completed nine hundred pages, he realized he had only just begun.

Then one night in 1867, somehow a smouldering fire flared up. It crept, then leaped along the floors and up the doorways. It burned into his office before anyone smelled the smoke.

The Indian servants rushed to the now burning office. They knew whatever Mariano was doing must be important. They threw books and bundles of papers out the window. They saved most of the records, but the nine hundred pages were burned to ashes.

Casa Grande was gone. Mariano felt too discouraged to start again. He gave up the project. Back he went to his gardens, always a place to work out troubles.

Years before, he had imported thousands of grape cuttings. Now his grapes and wines won medals at all the fairs. Garden clubs asked him to speak. Visitors enjoyed the tours through the old barracks where he stored the wines.

His fruit trees bore as well as the grapevines. One summer Francisca was away. Mariano sent her a letter begging her to come home. He said he had been picking peaches every day. Now they were stacked in every room in the house!

Mariano's family gave him more and more grandchildren each year. The governor's toast at Mariano's and Francisca's wedding so many years ago was coming true. Just one thing remained to complete Mariano's dream, but that would keep for now. Right now his vines, his trees and his children were the most important to him.

CHAPTER 21

Mariano Finishes His Story

THEN THE THING HE HAD HOPED FOR SO long, his famous wish, came true. At the long-ago Fourth of July celebration he had praised Washington. People had laughed at his dream of riding on a train across the continent. In May, 1869, the historic gold spike joined the rails from each side of the United States.

Fanny (Epifania) and her husband decided to ride the train to Washington, D.C., on business. Grandpa Mariano went along to help her with her eight small children.

They didn't give him much time to write about the trip.

I tried to help Fanny . . . with all their family which is very large and too young to care for themselves alone. We travel swiftly by day and night, of course, but very comfortable.

His greatest love now was for his family. When the children were little, he had often had to be away. Once when a brother died, he went to help the family. Alone with eight children, Francisca had written:

GUADALUPE:

Come, come, come, come, come. You say that you love me very much and all our children. . . . Now at present my family needs your counsel. There is not one, not two, but many of us. . . . Come and guide your family. I myself cannot take care of everything . . . and big Benicia sends you many *embrazas*, many little kisses.

Much love,
BENICIA

"We travel swiftly by day and night, of course, but very comfortable."

Now the tables were turned. Francisca visited her daughters often, caring for new grandbabies. The winter after Mariano rode the train, she stayed in Fanny's home in Vallejo. Fanny and her family were still in New York. No children were left at *Lachryma Montis*, the youngest girls being in school in Benicia. Mariano felt the loneliness.

He wrote often to Francisca. One letter said in part:

Every day I ventilate [the house] opening the windows. . . . As soon as afternoon comes, I close the windows of your room and I go down to mine without anything else to do than read or write or make verses . . .

Another letter said:

I am so alone in this lovely place. . . . By nature I like company, educated and refined company. I don't like to to be the one who does all the talking. . . . La Isadora is washing my clothes. Tomorrow I shall iron everything except the shirts.

La Isadora was Chief Solano's eighty-nine-year-old widow.

In a letter to Platón that same winter, Mariano told what a lovely day it had been. He had eaten dinner at his brother Salvador's:

We dined on goose, very well stuffed with red *chile*, good bread, a bottle of wine and for dessert, a frying pan full of excellent beans *a la Mejicana*, tea and water.

Mariano complained of being alone. His grandchildren lived in other towns. A little boy, Jacobino, lived near him, though. He adored Mariano and visited him every day. Mariano drew pictures of a train for him — engine, cars, and caboose.

Jacobino liked the pictures and the verses Mariano wrote to go with them. He called Mariano *"patrón"* and Francisca *"patrona."* Sometimes he found maple sugar cubes and chocolate in his *patrón*'s pockets. Once he said he didn't like the *patrona* — she left the *patrón* alone too much!

Grandpa Mariano also wrote letters to his grandchildren. One letter went to Platón's four-year-old daughter, Felipa. He knew Platón would have to read it, so he wrote some extra news:

> *Abuela* says she can't write with her hurt wrist. . . .
> *Abuela* went into the yard where the cows are. . . .
> When she finished milking . . . she went close to the creature . . . patting her on the back. All of a sudden
> . . . the cow gave her a kick. . . . Poor *Abuela* fell . . . and broke her wrist.

Then he tells her about the hills covered with trees:

> In those hills there are bears, deer, coyotes and rabbits . . . and quails and robins, and rattlesnakes which are very poisonous. . . . Also there are other kinds of animals called *squatters.*

After complaining about how the squatters steal fences, lambs, horses and milk from the cows, he says:

> *Abuelo* curses them in Spanish because he doesn't know how to do it in English.

One Christmas, Francisca had gone to see their daughter, Maria. She and her little boy were sick. Mariano missed Francisca, but wrote and said he didn't know what Maria would do without her.

You know mothers are always the comfort of their daughters. . . . Mamas are the ones who provide sympathy ("who are the cloth for tears" as is said). Take good care of them, pet them, for often that does more good than medicine; nonetheless science . . . is necessary and very comforting when one has faith in the doctor.

Later in the same letter, Mariano comments on their son Andronico's manners. Andronico has not answered his mother's letter promptly.

. . . when one receives a letter from a mother, he ought to be courteous, deferential and . . . respectful to her. To a stranger, no matter who he may be, one answers a letter with the penalty, if he doesn't do it, of being considered badly "brought up" — good education and Society require it.

Mariano had thought the only writing he would do now would be to his family and friends. But many people urged him to start his history again. Then a man came to see him. He said the California historian, Hubert H. Bancroft, wanted Mariano to work with him. It took several months to persuade Mariano to start writing again. He had kept his records, but the loss of the nine hundred pages still hurt.

Once again, he put down on paper everything he could remember or had records for. The one book he thought he would write turned into five. All of this was in Spanish, of course.

Bancroft translated much of Mariano's writings into English. In his many-volumned *History of California* he quotes Mariano G. Vallejo often.

One March afternoon in 1882, sounds of music wound through the streets of Sonoma. Behind the band came scores of friends and neighbors. The parade stopped in front of *Lachryma Montis*.

When Francisca and Mariano came to the door, cries of "Happy Fiftieth Wedding Anniversary!" greeted them. The group poured into the house to join the children and grandchildren.

Luisa sang, there were many speeches, and a gold-headed cane was given to Mariano.

In the fifty years of their marriage, Francisca had kept her good looks. She and Mariano still made a handsome couple as they received everyone's warm wishes.

The little boy in Monterey who had wanted to stay and fight for his home had come a long way. At first, he had thought pirates and Indians were his enemies. When Spain ignored the new land, he welcomed the Mexican government. Working for the storekeepers opened his eyes to a larger world. A concerned governor opened his mind. Reading his fine collection of books gave him an exceptional education.

From the Russians he learned respect for his workers. The petty quarreling of the *Californios* worried him. The acceptance of California as a state was the promise of a real future for his beloved land.

He could understand how the Indians had felt at

being pushed from their lands. But he wouldn't complain. If some laws of the new flag's government seemed harsh, they made for a glowing future.

He alone, of his boyhood companions, had had a part in making his dreams come true. Juan Alvarado and José Castro had chosen politics as their way of life. Both had been governors under the Mexican flag. Both had been active in the revolt of the *Californios*. But when the Americans took over, Castro left for Mexico and Alvarado took no part in the new state's government.

Mariano spent his last years contentedly among his large family and friends. He died in 1890 at home in Sonoma.

The schools were closed and the flags were at half-mast in his honor. Of the four flags that had waved over his home, the last would truly keep its promise to protect and enrich his California.

Epilogue

THE SONOMA MISSION, GENERAL MARIano Guadalupe Vallejo's *Lachryma Montis*, barracks, and Petaluma Adobe are in the Sonoma State Historic Park. This is a part of the California State Park System. The buildings are open to the public almost every day of the year.

The shady, tree-lined drive welcomes today's visitors as it did in Mariano's time. His own room is on the right as one enters the house. Many of his personal belongings still furnish the home.

Across the courtyard, past the still-flowing fountain is the Swiss Chalet. The State made this into a museum, with a Park staff attendant to answer questions.

Further down the main street, the tree-filled plaza contains a bust of the General. The barracks are across the street. Just beyond, to the east, stands the partially restored mission.

Twenty minutes away is the Petaluma Adobe, one of the largest *adobe* buildings remaining in California. Here one can see the candle-dipping room, the looms on the balcony and the Vallejos' private quarters. In the courtyard is the huge kettle used for melting the tallow for the candles. Chickens roam around the old *carreta*.

Park officials have provided picnic grounds below the building beside the creek.

Special school tours and other groups come here throughout the year. Advance notice is appreciated by the State Park Headquarters in Sonoma.

The Russian River empties into the Pacific Ocean midway between Bodega Bay on the south, and Fort Ross, thirteen miles north on State Highway 1. Part of the Fort has been restored as a State Historical Monument, much as Mariano saw it. Fire, by accident and by arson, has damaged the buildings several times. The Commander's house, the Russian Orthodox Chapel, and the block houses surround the picnic area.

Sutter's Fort, also a State Historical Monument, houses a museum in Sacramento, still the capital of California.

Sources for Quotations

Page 4. Bancroft, Hubert Howe. *History of California*, Vol. II, p. 230.
Page 41. Vallejo, Mariano Guadalupe, *Historia de California*, MS, Vol. II, p. 190.
Page 109. Bari, Valeska. *The Course of Empire*, pp. 55, 56.
Pages 78, 79, 81, 83, 84, 85, 109, 113, 114, 127, 128, 129, 130, and 131. Emparan, Madie Brown. *Vallejos of California*, pp. 35, 36, 38, 87, 117, 118, 119, 204, 290, and 330.

Bibliography

Atherton, Gertrude. *Golden Gate Country*. N.Y.: Duell, Sloan & Pearce, 1945.

——— *Splendid Idle Forties*. N.Y.: Frederick A. Stokes Co., 1902.

Bancroft, Hubert H., ed. *History of California*. S.F.: The History Company of San Francisco, 1884–1890.

Bari, Valeska, ed. *The Course of Empire*. N.Y.: Coward-McCann, Inc., 1931.

Bean, Walton. *California: An Interpretive History*. N.Y.: McGraw-Hill Book Co., 1973.

Beck, Warren A., and Haase, Ynez. *Historical Atlas of California*. Norman: University Press of Oklahoma, 1974.

Bauer, Helen. *California Indian Days*. Garden City: Doubleday and Co., 1968.

——— *California Mission Days*. Garden City: Doubleday and Co., 1951.

——— *California Rancho Days*. Garden City: Doubleday and Co., 1953.

Buell, Robert K. *California Stepping Stones*. Palo Alto: Stanford University Press, 1948.

Caughey, John W. *California*. N.Y.: Prentice Hall, Inc., 1940.

Chester, Michael. *Forts of Old California*. N.Y.: Putnam, 1967.

Clairmonte, Glenn. *John Sutter of California*. N.Y.: Thomas Nelson Sons, 1954.

Cleland, Robert. *Cattle on a Thousand Hills*. San Marino: Huntington Library, 1941.

Corle, Edwin. *The Royal Highway*. N.Y.: Duell, Sloan & Pearce, 1949.

Dakin, Susanna. *Lives of William Hartnell*. Palo Alto: Stanford University Press, 1949.

Dutton, Davis, ed. *Missions of California*. N.Y.: Ballantine Books, 1972.

Emparan, Madie Brown. *Vallejos of California*. S.F.: Gleeson Library Association, University of San Francisco, 1968.

Erskine, Dorothy W. *Big Ride*. N.Y.: Crowell, 1958.

Garner, William. *Letters from California 1846–1847*. Edited by Donald M. Craig. Berkeley: University of California Press, 1970.

Hansen, Harvey, and Jeanne Thurlow Millar. *Wild Oats in Eden: Sonoma County in the 1900's*. Santa Rosa: Hansen & Millar, 1962.

Ide, William B. *Bear Flagger*. S.F.: John Howell Books, 1962.

138

Lewis, Oscar. *Sea Routes to the Gold Fields*. N.Y.: Alfred A. Knopf, Inc., 1949.

———— *Sutter's Fort: Gateway to the Gold Fields*. N.Y.: Prentice Hall, Inc., 1966.

Lothrop, Marian Lydia. "Indian Campaigns of General M. G. Vallejo." *Society of California Pioneers Quarterly* Vol. IX, No. 3, September 1932.

McKittrick, Myrtle. *Vallejo, Son of California*. Portland: Binfords and Mort, 1944.

Norton, Henry K. *The Story of California*. Chicago: A. C. McClurg and Co., 1921.

Powell, Emily Brown. "A Modern Knight." *Harpers Magazine*, April 1893.

Roberts, Helen M. *Mission Tales: Big Chief Solano*. Palo Alto: Stanford University Press, 1948.

Scott, Mel. *San Francisco Bay Area*. Berkeley: University of California Press, 1966.

Smilie, Robert S. *The Sonoma Mission*. Fresno: Valley Publishers, 1975.

White, Stewart Edward. *Ranchero*. Garden City: Doubleday, Doran and Co., 1933.

Index

This book was designed and produced by Dave Comstock.
The text type is Palatino and was composed by Dwan Typography.
The display type and initials are Berling Roman and Berling Italic.
Printed by Thomson-Shore, Inc.

About the Author: Esther Jacoby Comstock was born in San Francisco shortly before the 1906 earthquake and fire. When the ashes settled, her banker father moved his family across the bay to Oakland, where she received her early education. She attended the University of California at Berkeley for two years before transferring to the College of the Pacific at Stockton. In 1926 she received her B.A. and teaching credential, and married architect Floyd B. Comstock. Not until her third (and youngest) child was attending the same college did she finally pursue a teaching career.

For ten years she taught primary grades, and then continued for five years as a substitute teacher, mostly in the fourth grade. From this experience came her desire to improve the quality of California history books available to young people. Her first book, *Vallejo and the Four Flags,* is used in hundreds of California and Nevada public and private schools as a supplementary text in the study of California history. Esther Comstock also wrote *Feliciana's California Miracle,* the fascinating true story about a young widow who accompanied Juan Bautista de Anza's colonizing expedition to California in 1775–1776. Feliciana Gutiérrez de Arballo, the heroine of that story, became the matriarch of a great California family, and her granddaughter married Mariano Vallejo.

About the Illustrator: Floyd B. Comstock was born in Chico, California, in 1902. He grew up in Oakland and Hayward, and in 1924 graduated from the School of Architecture at the University of California at Berkeley. He practiced architecture for fifty years in San Francisco and Walnut Creek, and took up painting when he retired. In addition to his California watercolors, he has painted and sketched in Alaska, Mexico, Spain, South American, the Caribbean and the South Pacific.